I step into his arms, and we dance slowly. My head finds its way onto his shoulder. I feel his heart beating, his hand pressing the small of my back. Being with Michael, feeling him close like this, feels natural. But then, I tell myself, maybe he's had practice. "So do you take all the girls out here?"

"No," he says into my hair. "No girls. Just one woman."

Woman. To be thought of as a woman, the one thing that every girl takes for granted that she'll be, and that I thought I'd never have a chance to become.

I can't help it, I feel something new. Tell me if I'm crazy. Here I am, in a country and a city I've never been in before, in the arms of a man I barely know, and I feel like I've come home, like I belong right here, right now. With him.

Michael leans into me and gives me the softest, most gentle kiss, like petals. It's very chaste, in a way—totally respectful, almost old-fashioned, as if he's asking permission for something more that we both know is coming. No boundaries are crossed.

But, somehow, they all are.

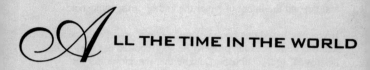

ALL THE TIME IN THE WORLD

LIZ NICKLES

HarperEntertainment
An Imprint of HarperCollins Publishers

HarperEntertainment

An Imprint of HarperCollins*Publishers*
10 East 53rd Street, New York, NY 10022

ISBN 0-380-81076-X

HarperCollins®, ■®, and HarperEntertainment™ are trademarks of HarperCollins Publishers Inc.

A version of this book was printed in 1999 by Avon Books.

First HarperEntertainment Printing: October 2000

Printed in the United States of America

Visit HarperEntertainment on the
World Wide Web at www.harpercollins.com

00 01 02 03 04 OPM 10 9 8 7 6 5 4 3 2

To the real Nicole

Acknowledgments

This book would not have been possible in any way without Todd Harris, a brilliant friend and consummate professional who encouraged it from the very first thought. Thank you, Todd. Much gratitude is also due to Tia Maggini, Avon Books, and the unstoppable Nick Ellison. I also wish to thank Todd Black, Jason Blumenthal, and Columbia Pictures for their support. And special thanks to the multi-talented Jennifer Love Hewitt, who shared the inspiration that was the spirit of the real Nicki.

Prologue

I *have to close my eyes now, like the shutter of a
camera, so I'll never forget this moment. Yes, I
feel it: the wind whips my long hair; it stings my
face and tangles in my mouth, which is open, screaming, laughing. Far below, curling into the base of the
cliff, is the Aegean Sea, warm and beckoning. And
he is beside me, holding my hand.*

*"I can't do it." How can I jump? I don't like cliffs.
I don't like heights. I don't like surprises—I'm particularly adverse to killer drops, sharp rocks, and
schools of sharks that are no doubt circling exactly
where I will splash down.*

"Yes you can." The guy is persistent.

"I can't." I pull back. I'm not ready.

"I see bravery," he says.

Brave? Me?

1

"I can't do it."

"Yes you can. We've done it before. You can do it."

He takes my hand and strokes it.

"I'm afraid," I whisper.

"Hold my hand."

I grip as tightly as I can.

"One, two . . . you're going with me, right, Nick?"

"Right." The wind drowns out my voice. Can he hear me?

"We're going together," he says. The reassurance of his voice makes it OK somehow.

I take a deep, deep breath. I want to remember this moment, never lose it.

I hold his hand, and we jump.

And then I am falling in the sunlight. It's a long way down, but I'm not alone. He's there, still holding my hand. If someone's holding you up, can you ever really fall?

"We're going together, right?"

Right. I'm flying now, somewhere between the earth, the sky, and the sea. Holding his hand and flying.

Some people say that when you die, that's it: the ultimate alone. You're born alone, you die alone. That's what they say.

Well, they're wrong.

Because when you are in love, and when you are loved, you're not alone. Not ever.

I know. And now I will tell you how.

Chapter 1

When you are twenty-one years old and about to graduate from college, you've got a lot of things on your mind, but dying isn't one of them.

Let's face it: I don't have time to die. When am I going to squeeze it in? Between my internship interviews with law firms? Before I give the valedictory speech? At 2 A.M., after I've finished waiting tables? Or maybe I should cancel my date with Tim tonight, my only semblance of a social life. I don't think so.

Had I for one second seriously thought I was dying, I would never have scheduled all this. I would have made other plans, or, should I say, no plans. Maybe that's why I've chosen to ignore these headaches for so long. I have too much to do to take them seriously. You can tell yourself *OK, you're not dying, are you?* And you can take an Extra-Strength Tylenol and forget it, or try to.

At the end of your senior year, you have a lot to contend with. There's not just graduation, there's moving out of your old place, moving into a new one, the internship interviews, the good-byes, the whole new start thing.

I can't say I'll miss the apartment. I think I was mentally packed to leave before I even moved in two years ago. If Emily hadn't already had the lease, I would probably never have moved in. It's in a convenient part of Evanston, not far from the campus, but it's a soulless place: low ceilings, ground (aka "garden") floor, wood floors that haven't seen a sander in decades. The furniture came from Emily's grandmother's coach house; we just threw sheets over everything so we wouldn't have to look at it. But, since Emily, Eric, Tim, and I lived there, it was home. It's hard to believe we're splitting up, but Eric's pre-med, Tim's got a job downtown with an architecture firm, Em's going to New York to open a boutique, and I'm hoping my internship will come through before I start law school in the fall.

Tim and I are going on four years now—we're like an old married couple. No surprises there.

Em and Eric are a couple, too, but of another sort. They have a lot in common: Em's looking for the perfect guy, and so is Eric. So far, neither of them has found him. Tim and I are getting a place together in Printer's Row, which is like the Soho of Chicago. Or almost. Em and Eric are on their own, but I'll miss them. Who will dress me? Together they formed a wardrobe committee and helped me pull together a professional image so I'd make the right impression at Avery, Gardener and Brown. Eric found the navy suit in a secondhand shop. Em did my makeup. When I looked in the mirror this morning, I was five-foot six, a hundred fifteen pounds, my light brown hair pulled back uncharacteristically smooth and sleek in a tortoiseshell barrette, hazel eyes shadowed just so, and Em's real pearl studs rounding out the picture. I looked, in short, like a lawyer, which was exactly the desired effect. The question is, did I act like a lawyer in the interview? Did I make them believe in my capabilities?

I had the headache in the interview, but I always seem to have the headache these days. I had it this morning when I woke up, I had it yesterday when I was packing, and last night while I was polishing my valedictory speech. But stress'll do that to you: take two aspirin and call me in the morning.

So now I'm heading back to the apartment. I'm still in the street, but I can already hear the music coming from the place. If the lady upstairs hadn't been hard of hearing, we would've been evicted long ago. Emily is to blame: she believes that any event is cause for celebration. The Cubs game is blaring simultaneously—a necessity, in order to hear it over the music. Opening the door to the apartment is an aural assault.

"So, Nick, how'd it go?" Eric is blessed with a voice that is louder than either the speakers or the TV. It will come in handy for shouting "Code Blue!" in his new career. He doesn't look like a doctor—yet. At least I've never seen a black doctor with a shaved head, a tattoo, and an earring.

Can I shout loud enough? "I think it went OK—but who knows? It was like talking to Mount Rushmore." I glance at Tim, whose eyes never waver from the screen. Seventh inning, two outs, Cubs up. So much for Tim. We have a relationship, but you have to be realistic.

Eric shrugs. "Well, what'd you expect? They're lawyers."

"Correction. They're Avery, Gardener and Brown, the premier environmental lawyers in the country. They don't have to talk." I wish they'd turn down the music. My head is pounding along with the bass. I drop onto Tim's lap and rub his blonde hair.

"So you did good, huh?" Blue eyes finally wrench themselves away from the screen. I squeeze his arm: the man has some biceps.

"I blew them away with my editorial. They couldn't believe that I was actually published in the *Tribune*."

"So how much did you ask them for?"

"Come on, Tim, I think you got it backwards— it's a summer internship. The serious bucks are after law school."

Eric hands me a beer. "Well, that's nothing. It'll be close to ten years before I'm making a living."

Emily swoops upon us, a vision in black, her orange-streaked blonde hair spiked unmercifully, her cigarette slicing the air with a trail of smoke. Ashes scatter as she waves her hands. "Nobody told you to go to med school. You could have been a vet."

"It takes the same amount of time." Eric shrugs.

"Dogs are people, too!" Em notes, as she frequently does.

"Fine. You be a vet."

We've been there before. Tim ignores them. He frowns at me. "Well, you still should have asked them for the dollar amount. An interview isn't all about them. You need to know. You'll have that monster loan to pay off."

"Don't remind me."

Emily's cigarette smoke wafts in my direction. "Why don't you just break down and ask your parents to help out?"

Before I can strangle her, Eric cuts in. "We don't want to go into that again."

Luckily, the phone rings. My relationship with my parents is not a topic I relish, at least not since their divorce, a time frame that covers about a fourth of my life. From the moment my mother and father split up, it's never been easy to think about us as a family, mainly because we haven't been one. Emily grabs the phone. Emily grabs any chance to grab the phone. Within seconds, she's gesturing in my direction with one set of blue-black-polished fingernails and, with the other, motioning Tim to turn down the TV and the music.

"It's for you!"

I'm exhausted. I really don't want to deal with anyone right now. "Tell them I'm not here."

Emily arches her eyebrows. "Believe me, you are here." She thrusts the phone into my hands. As soon as he speaks, I recognize the Boston tones of Arnold Gardener, whom I just left about an hour ago.

"Yes, Mr. Gardener. This is Nicole."

During this conversation, I almost forget my headache. Mr. Gardener uses words like "opportunity," "vision," and "human resources." This has to be it—the offer.

I tell him how much I admire the direction in which the firm is heading, how much I'd like to be on the team. And suddenly, it's within my grasp, everything I've worked for for four years. I see my name on the letterhead, on the office door, on their card. I see my future.

"Thank you, Mr. Gardener. Thanks for calling."

Eric, Emily, and Tim leap into action.

"So?" demands Tim.

"So?"

"So?"

It's a chorus.

"So . . ." I smile, savoring the moment. Then I throw myself into Tim's arms. "So, they want me!"

Chapter 2

*T*he Pink Cadillac is the kind of place that tries to re-create a nostalgia that probably never existed in the first place. I wasn't around for the Fifties, but if there was a place like this, decked out in mirror-finish chrome, Formica, and red vinylette booths, it was probably on the set of an Elvis film. But it's a fun place to hang, and the tips are always pretty good, so working here hasn't been too bad, in spite of the fact that I have to wear a poodle skirt and saddle shoes. Oh yes—the poodle skirt is micro-mini length, so there is some evolution acknowledged. The best part is, this is the place where I met Emily and Eric four years ago. Emily, of course, was a customer. She's never had to work. Eric was a star manager-slash-performer. I tell him he always got the biggest tips because he was the biggest ham. Anyhow, I had just started as a waitress when I dropped a tray of chocolate and strawberry shakes into Emily's lap. Emily being Emily, she threatened to sue, claiming I had ruined her new Prada bag. Eric stepped in. The first thing he did was to apologize for my clumsiness, and the second thing he did was to pick up the purse and lick it clean. By the end, we were all laughing hysterically, Emily forgot about the lawsuit, and we were new best friends.

I think the reason we all get along so well is we're so different. Nobody even tries to understand anybody else. Growing up in J. Crew Wilmette, I'd never come across anybody like Emily, with her daily-changing hair color, wall-to-wall vintage wardrobe, and total commitment to every animal short of roadkill. For six weeks, we sheltered a raccoon she picked up on the edge of the forest preserve, until it escaped from our dorm window. And Eric, who has a comment for every occasion, became our unofficial den mother. It was only natural that we get an apartment together, and we've been roommates for two years now.

Tonight is my last night hostessing at the Pink Cadillac, so I'm allowing myself to get a little bit nostalgic as I pull my hair into the prerequisite ponytail. "It's going to be funny not having these guys around," I say to Tim.

"Yeah, but maybe we'll have some privacy for once." He kisses me on the neck, just a peck. Tim is subletting a place in Old Town from a cousin who's moving to Washington. "Besides, they'll drop by constantly. They're not capable of functioning without us. Now get out your calendar."

I rummage in my backpack for my Palm Pilot, a graduation gift from my father. The problem is finding the time to put all the information I need into it. But I have to admit, it's a useful gadget. Tim and I are all about calendars these days.

"Shoot."

"The lease starts in two weeks. Can we be out of here and in the new place by then?"

"I'm already packed."

"Great. I've scheduled the first weekend for cleaning and painting. My cousin is leaving his furniture. It's ugly, but it's cheap. I've made up a spreadsheet for us, covering each of our costs."

Tim is even more organized than I am. He has our entire future planned, right down to the IRAs. Two control freaks: that's what we have in common. I always say Tim saved me from the brink of oblivion because I met him when my laptop broke down and almost took my entire existence with it. I was sitting in the library, banging futilely on the keyboard, when Tim came over and managed to get into both my hard drive and my life. Tim's the kind of guy who, when nobody's had time to do the wash in two weeks and we're living out of the hamper, emerges from the closet in a freshly pressed pink button-down shirt, which is exactly what he does now.

"Do we have to deal with spreadsheets right now? I'm going to be late for work." I grab my angora sweater and head for the door. Tonight's the big graduation party. The place is going to be a zoo.

Tim shrugs. "OK, later." Then he smiles. "Tonight, we celebrate."

"You celebrate, you mean. I work."

When we walk into the Pink Cadillac, the place is packed, and it's not even seven o'clock. Every booth is bulging, and there's a line out the door. Jennifer, the girl whose shift is ending, gives me an "I'm out of here" look, and I brace myself and assume my position, clipboard in hand. In the center of the main dining room, surrounded by the red vinylette booths, is a 1956 Eldorado convertible with the seats removed, which also serves as a stage. Eric is dancing there now with Gigi, the disc jockey. At about two hundred fifty pounds, stuffed into a Day-Glo muumuu, Gigi is a fair match for Eric as they rock to "My Boyfriend's Back."

"Nicki!" I spot Emily, over in a booth, waving frantically. She's wearing a black Gucci jumpsuit and a thrift shop jacket of fake leopard. She jumps up from her seat, races over to Gigi, grabs the microphone, and jumps onto the Eldorado's hood. "Everybody, I have an announcement to make. Our favorite hostess, the Pink Cadillac's own Nicki McBain, has just been hired by Avery, Gardener and Brown!" She lets out a whoop, and the entire crowd cheers.

"Nicki!" yells Gigi, "Come on down! Everybody, let's give our little Nicki chick a big send-off into the cold, hard legal world!"

I duck and look for a place to hide, but Eric drags me up to the Caddy.

"I don't get paid enough for this!" I shout.

"Come on, Nick, have some fun for a change!" He lifts me up onto the hood.

"I'm gonna get you guys for this!"

"Who's your Mama!" screams Gigi into the mike.

"You're our Mama!" the crowd shouts back.

The music slams into "Twist and Shout," and Tim jumps up onto the hood with us, then Emily. We all put our arms around each other's shoulders and dance in a circle.

I wake up the next morning with a headache. Who wouldn't. It was one long night. But when you're spending the last night of your undergrad life working at something you hope to never do again, and you're about to start something that's going to become the thing you do for the rest of your life, you deserve to celebrate, don't you?

I try to forget the headache while I put the finishing touches on my speech for the graduation ceremonies. It took me three weeks to write the valedictory speech, which will last approximately ten minutes. I keep thinking of Lincoln and the Gettysburg Address—it was short and perfect, and nobody ever forgot it. That's the way I'd like my speech to be.

Standing in front of the bathroom mirror, putting on my makeup, I practice again. And again. I know I have to finish packing, but I can't even think about the Old Town apartment and Tim's spreadsheet until later today, when graduation is finally over.

Eric sticks his head in. "Pro-ject!" He sings the word like an opera phrase. "Diaphragm!"

"I believe they will have a microphone."

"Need help packing?"

I shake my head and continue to mouth the words of my speech.

"My dad's coming by to help me with the boxes. Your parents stopping over?"

Parents. Stopping over. I sigh in spite of myself. "Yes, they are. I think. Last I heard, my mother hung up on Dad's wife."

"Wonder Woman versus Batgirl. Stay tuned."

"It's getting to be a bit of a boring rerun." The story is always the same: Dad is coming. He really is this time. Really. What time should he be there? He can't wait to see me, neither can Kate and Justin. Now, what time should he be there again? Fast forward to whatever time that is. Dad doesn't show up. He's sorry, he's so sorry, but something came up. I understand, don't I? End of episode. Till next time. Then there's my mother. She's never exactly warmed to having been dumped for a younger woman, and I can't say I blame her, but how long can I listen to her problems with my father? The marriage counselor never could figure it out, so how can I? Where does that leave me? Precisely in the middle: "Tell your mother this." "Tell your father that."

Then there's Kate. Aside from the fact that she wrecked my mother's and my life, she's pretty innocuous. I think she read some psycho-babble

19

books on stepparenting, because she's always talking about wanting to "share" with me, and she does obvious stuff like give me a present whenever she sees me. When I was younger, my relationship with Kate was akin to an all-out war. I tried my best to oust her from the scene, but it always seemed to backfire. Now that she has presented my father with a son and heir, it looks like she's here to stay. On the rare times that my dad does show up, he always sits next to Kate, making me feel like a third wheel.

Forget it. I put myself through school. I got myself into law school next fall. I'll figure out how to pay for it somehow over the next twenty years. They do their thing, I do mine.

Suddenly I see a black blur in the mirror: Emily collapsing onto the bed, still in the outfit she wore last night.

"Oh my God." Em flings an arm over her face, as if the sun would melt her mascara, or what's left of it that isn't smeared across her cheeks. "What time is it? I'm never gonna be ready for the ceremonies."

Eric smirks. "You're such a slut."

"Shut up. What do you know about a woman's needs? I may never see Brian again. Nick, what time is your speech?"

"In fifty-four minutes. Tim already left. He's on the committee."

"Can you make it an hour and a half?"

"Sorry."

But of course, she'll be there. Em's always been there for me, ever since the day I milk-shaked her purse. Her life has been so different from mine, with a wealthy family and boarding schools, Europe and horses, but we've both been on our own a lot, and we know what that's all about. So even though we're nothing alike, we feel like we're sisters.

I might as well put on the cap and gown now. I think I'm putting it off till the last minute because graduation seems so final. After four years of total togetherness, Emily, Eric, Tim, and I are breaking up our little family. Em and Eric are like the brother and sister I never had. Well, actually I have a brother, a half brother, to be exact. Justin. He's four years old, but I can't say we're close. In fact, I hardly know him. And—does this sound awful?—I'm not sure I want to. Having your father replace you with a new baby isn't easy, even if you're almost grown yourself. Em says it's irrational to be competitive with a nursery-schooler, but I can't seem to help it. I can't forget all those times my father wasn't there for me when I was little. Dad worked nights, weekends, whatever it took. He traveled constantly and never took us with him. Now that he's remarried—to Kate, his former administrative assistant, who quit her job the second she became the second Mrs. McBain—he's seen the light and become a poster parent to Justin. Never misses a sandbox date or a kindergarten interview. He even took a Daddy and Me class with the kid on Saturdays. No wonder I have a headache.

A huge bouquet appears in front of my face in the mirror: yellow daffodils, my favorite. Tim wraps me in his arms. "For my favorite valedictorian." He leans in from behind for a kiss, his silky blond hair as pale as the daffodils. Tim and I are one of those constants of life. We just go on and on. Ever since my laptop crisis that first year of school, neither of us has ever had to think about dating or relationships since, which is great when you barely have time to go out in the first place. Tim, Emily, and Eric—they're my family. I don't like to think about what's going to happen now that we're all moving on to do our own things. It's the worst part of graduating, but at least I know Tim and I will be together.

In the mirror, I see a flurry of activity in the bedroom behind me. Emily is trying to redesign the classic graduation gown, adding a belt, jewelry. Tim hovers over my shoulder to position his cap and tassel.

"The cap and gown: the great equalizer," he says. "Everybody looks like a jerk."

"Speak for yourself," snorts Emily. She's swathed her cap in a veil. It's totally her. This woman is going to be a major force in fashion.

My head feels about ready to crack open, like an overcooked hard-boiled egg. I reach for the aspirin bottle and flip on the water to fill a glass. Everything seems shaky all of a sudden; the glass slips out of my hand and shatters all over the tile floor. Millions of little shards crunch underfoot as I try to steady myself on the sink.

"I'll get the Dustbuster," Tim says. "Concentrate on your speech."

Not possible, but I'll try.

"Nick," calls Eric over the whine of the Dustbuster, "Your mom's here."

Amazing. She actually made it without being detained by a closing. I give my hair one last pat, smoothing it over my shoulders. Do I look different today, my last day as a college student? Same navy-blue eyes, same fair skin, same mouth that never looks good with lipstick, but today I'll try anyway. I carefully outline my lips and brush on a burgundy color. My hand shakes and it smears. I blot it off. Forget it.

"Hello, darling." My mother is shorter than me and very put-together. She wears very tailored pantsuits and always has some kind of co-ordinating scarf around her neck. Today the pantsuit is white and the scarf is pastel. Actually, I've always thought my mother was much prettier than I am. I'm like a dark-haired, watercolor version of her—edges blurred, features softer and less dramatic.

"Hi, Mom." How many people can fit into a bathroom? "You made it. No closings?"

"Nicole, do you think I wouldn't be here to celebrate with my brilliant daughter?" She hands me a small package. "This is for today."

"Mom, I'm in a hurry."

"Here, I'll help you." She rips off the paper herself. "Look, honey." She opens the box and fishes out a gold charm bracelet.

"Thank you, Mom." It's not really my kind of thing, but she's trying in the way she usually does, by giving me something she'd like to have. I'm her daughter, but I don't think she really knows who I am. She was too busy fighting my father to really get to know me.

"It was mine. Look—this one's my graduation charm." She grabs my wrist and clips on the bracelet. It jingles when I move my arm.

Emily barges in and grabs my arm. "That is fantastic, Lori, isn't it, Nick?"

"Yes, so—retro." It's the best I can do.

The fashion queen having spoken, Em drops my arm and disappears.

Mom laughs, but she knows I'm not into the bracelet. "I guess it's not that stylish anymore, but it means a lot to me. I want you to have it."

"Thanks, Mom. It'll go with my poodle skirt."

As soon as she turns away, I unfasten the bracelet and tuck it into my pocket, under my graduation robe. It's not my kind of thing, and, besides, I don't want it jangling into the microphone during my speech.

We head back into the living room just as Dad, Kate, and Justin are arriving. Dad's his usual self—suit, trademark bow tie, no gray in his slicked-back hair, in a hurry to leave before he's even come in. Kate is taller than Dad, thin, Armani suited. She's had her platinum blonde hair cut stylishly short, and a barrette holds back her bangs. Justin is a force of nature. He explodes into the place, leaping onto the couch, jumping up and down, a tornado in a buzz cut, looking for something to wreck.

"Nicki!" Dad booms out. "My class valedictorian! Honey, we are so proud!" He gives me a bear hug. Over my shoulder, he notices Mom and nods at her politely. "Lori."

Mom inclines her chin an inch. "Dan."

It amazes and frightens me how after a marriage of fifteen years, sleeping together some five thousand nights, and the joint production of a child, a relationship can be reduced to a nod.

"I hope we're not late," Kate says breathlessly. "We just got back from Barcelona last night. Justin's a little jet-lagged. Justin! Honey! Off the couch! Come here—I have your snack." She smiles and hands him cookies in a baggie and a juice box. "It's snack time in Barcelona."

"Snack attack!" Justin giggles as he leaps onto the juice box and gives it a ferocious squeeze. Grape juice spurts across the room and scores a direct hit on my mother's white jacket: bull's-eye.

"Oh my god! I am so sorry, aren't we, Justin? He just gets so excited when he sees his big sister. Is there any club soda? Club soda will take it right out."

"Sorry. All the supplies are packed," says Eric, who knows permanent damage when he sees it.

"Just send us the cleaning bill," offers Kate, making an unsuccessful grab for the juice box as Justin races by, waving it, streaking a purple wake. My mother dabs her jacket with a Kleenex and seethes, but waves her off. My father, an expert at issue avoidance, pretends nothing happened.

"I'll see you at the ceremonies, Nicki," Mom says, making a getaway.

"Dad, can't you control that kid?"

" 'That kid' happens to be your brother, Nicki. And you should have seen yourself when you were that age. You were always out of control."

"Like you were ever there to see," I snap. Somehow this always happens. One thing leads to another, and it snowballs. I really love my parents, but there are just so many problems involved, so many strings attached, so many past hurts on all sides that sometimes it's easier to just skip it. That's why I never asked them for money for college. A scholarship wasn't easy to get, and working after class was hardly fun, but all of it was easier than being the subject of their battles about who owes whom what.

Kate steps between us, smiling a bit too brightly. "So, do we have dinner plans for tonight?"

"I'm not really hungry."

"Nicki, dinner is six hours away."

"I have a headache."

"In six hours?"

I always have a headache these days. That much is true. And this isn't helping. I rub my head.

Dad pats my shoulder. "You've been pushing

yourself too hard. I don't see why . . ."

I guess that's the point. Since he met Kate, he doesn't see much, period, except her. And Justin. "Can we please change the subject?" I ask. At this rate, I'll forget what my speech is even about. "I gotta get going." What more is there to say? Well, maybe one more thing. "I've got the internship at AG&B."

The perfect exit line.

I'm standing at the podium, in the middle of my speech, making a point about our global commitment to the environment, when a giant fist reaches into my skull and squeezes like a vice. This is the worst one yet.

"As citizens of the earth, we are all joined in a special partnership to respect the land, each in our own way . . ."

I can't begin to imagine how this speech sounds to the people who are listening. All my careful researching, writing, and finessing, and now I'm reading the words off my cards just to get through it any way I can. My head feels like it's going to explode, and the writing on the cards is blurry. God, what a migraine. It's unbelievable. Somehow I sound out the syllables, like a child reciting a phonics lesson. I make it to the end. I hear the applause burst through the auditorium. The faces in front of me blend together in an indistinguishable mass.

"Thank you, Nicole McBain." The dean is standing next to me, shaking my hand.

"Thank you, Dean Crawford." I manage a smile and head toward my seat on the podium.

"And now, the graduating class of the year two thousand . . ."

The band picks up the school anthem. "Hail to purple, hail to white, hail to thee, Northwestern . . ."

The class erupts into cheers. Caps are flying as they are elatedly tossed into the air. I don't toss my cap. I feel very strange. A metallic taste fills my mouth, and I see two of everything. I've never fainted, but I feel as if I'm going to now. My knees give way. *What's happening?*

When I open my eyes, I'm staring up at a semicircle of worried faces. Emily is waving a program, fanning me. Dean Crawford is talking tensely into a cell phone.

"Where are the paramedics?" the dean is saying.

Paramedics? "I'm fine," I manage to say. God, this is so embarrassing, fainting on the stage at your own graduation. I have to get up.

Eric stops me. "Don't sit up too suddenly." He takes my pulse.

My mother's there, too. "What happened, Nicki? Did you fall?"

"It's stress," Emily announces firmly. "I've seen this before. One of the girls down the hall sophomore year. Fainted dead away. I feel like fainting myself. Do you want some water, Nick? How about a Tic-Tac?"

"She'll be fine," says Tim. I realize that he's holding my head in his lap.

The paramedics, in white coats, approach with a stretcher. A stretcher! They've got to be kidding. I immediately sit straight up.

"Clear the area, please," somebody says.

"This is ridiculous," I say. "It's just a headache."

"You fainted, Nicki," says Dean Crawford. "According to university policy, they have to look you over."

"Really, I'm fine," I plead.

"Of course you are," says the dean. "It's just a routine precaution." I can see he's thinking lawsuit.

The paramedics insist I get on the stretcher. I feel ridiculous but do it anyway. Eric keeps taking my pulse.

"Are you a doctor?" asks one of the paramedics.

"Well," says Eric, "any minute now."

The mass of people jamming the auditorium parts to let me and my entourage through. A few people who know me run over or call out something encouraging. I sit up, resisting the idea of lying limp like a sick person. Because I'm not, am I? Whatever I am, this experience is completely humiliating. We make our way to an emergency side exit and out to the street, where an ambulance is waiting curbside.

"I can walk."

"You have to lie down. Regulations."

I feel like I'm in an outtake from *E.R.* I'd just like to disappear. Instead, I try to resign myself to the situation as they ease me into the ambulance. Eric climbs in beside me; the ambulance doors close.

Chapter 3

I always knew I would have a graduation party; I just never thought it would happen in a hospital room. After holding me hostage for an entire day, the medical community is still refusing to cut me any slack. You'd think they'd forgotten their own graduations. Nothing here is important except blood work, blood work, blood work and blood work, until you pretty much run out of blood. Oh, and CAT scans. I had one of those, too.

Tim, Eric, and Emily have been great. Eric is my medical interface—he translates the doctors' jargon and has already become friends with the interns. Thanks to Eric, the cable TV was hooked up in my room within ten seconds. He was born to do this. Emily is wearing my hospital gown. She's really into that flapping-open back thing.

As for me, I refuse to wear it. That's for sick people. I'm wearing the vintage formal gown that I was going to wear to the dance Tim and I were supposed to go to last night. I might as well get my money's worth out of it. If they want to draw blood, they have to work their way around twenty yards of black tulle and a tiara. Eric's got the music pumped, and a bunch of our friends have stopped by. Gigi sent over a cake. Tim commandeered a bedpan and turned it into an ice bucket for the champagne, which was a graduation present from Em's uncle. So we're doing OK, considering the surroundings.

Em's modeling the hospital gown, flashing the flap back and forth. "Maybe I should carry these when I open my boutique."

"I'm going to be out of here any minute, so don't get too attached to the wardrobe," I note, sipping my paper cup of champagne.

Emily frowns. "I just wish they'd get their act together."

There is an undercurrent here that I prefer not to think about. Everything will be alright. Won't it?

All in all, my first two days here weren't so bad. It was the third day and today, the fourth, that have made me insane. By now I have no blood, or patience, left. It's hard to imagine what could take so long, but Eric explained about how hospitals move like glue over weekends and practically grind to a halt when it comes to holidays, and so we've been caught in the Memorial Day weekend backup at the labs. Only critical cases get attention over the holidays, Eric says, so at least whatever I have is probably not serious. That's what I'm hoping, but you never know. Being in a hospital makes you slightly sick, even if you weren't when you came in. You start to imagine things, like strange tropical illnesses that you might have picked up from contaminated fruit, or congenital defects that your body has harbored for years that are working their way to the surface. Or, at least, those are the kinds of thoughts I'm beginning to have, late at night, when I'm alone and can't sleep. You rationalize: if I'm still here, something has to be wrong. Then morning comes, and you shake it off. But, as the days pass, I have to admit, it becomes harder and harder to shake it off.

My friends have become bored with hanging out here, and I don't blame them. They have to get on with their lives. Our lease is up at the end of next week, and we have to move out of the apartment. Em and Eric have been pretty much stuck with the cleanup there, but they haven't complained. Tim has started working on our move to Old Town by himself, but I still have things to arrange and pack. I'm supposed to start my internship. God, what if this whatever-it-is drags on and affects my start date? Maybe AG&B won't wait for me, maybe they'll give the internship to somebody else while I sit here, a human pincushion in a bed with bars.

I hear my parents in the hall—both coming in at the same time. That's a novelty. They usually try to stagger their visits. They walk in together: even more unusual. No Kate. I immediately go on alert. Dr. Graham, who's been looking after me, walks in after them. Now I know—they're letting me out. Finally.

Mom comes right over to the head of the bed and sits on the side. Dad stares at the floor. Who won't he look at—me or Mom?

"So, I can leave, right?" I say to the doctor, not so much a question as a statement.

"Not exactly, Nicki. Listen to what I have to say very carefully."

"I'm listening."

"We got the results back from your CAT scan and all your blood work."

"And?"

"I wish there were an easier way to say this, but it's best to start with the facts."

"Facts?" Mom grips my shoulder, her nails digging right through the cloth of my T-shirt. Immediately I sense that these are not facts that I will want to hear. "What's going on?"

"Nicki, your neurological symptoms are due to the fact that you have a condition called neurofibromatosis, or NF2 for short.

"You've been experiencing slight symptoms for some time now, but the true nature of the situation indicates advanced stage activity."

"Are you saying I have a brain tumor?" He didn't say it, but I know it. I know it as sure as I'm sitting in this bed, in the way that you know things about yourself and the fiber of your body. Even when you don't want to believe it, you know it.

"It's not that simple, not black and white, but, essentially yes. I've spoken with your parents and they felt you'd want to know straight out."

I notice Dad. His hands are clenched into fists as he stares at the doctor. Mom is crying now.

"What you have is malignant, yes," Dr. Graham continues, "but it's also to some extent treatable."

"To what extent?" I ask, trying to absorb this.

"There are therapies . . ." He sticks up some X rays so I can get a better look at the assassin inside my head.

"But I feel fine. Are you sure? This can't be."

"Nicki, I wish it wasn't, but with this type of condition, the prognosis is unfortunately—guarded."

"This is—cancer?"

He nods.

I jump onto my knees in the bed. I can't help it—it's a reflex reaction. "So cut it out!" God, what am I saying?

"The tumor is too precarious to remove, and it's also metastasized. One thing we can do is slow things down with chemotherapy."

What is he saying? "Wait a minute. Are you telling me that this thing is going to kill me?"

The doctor shifts his weight. A good lawyer knows a hedge when she sees it. "Well, there have been cases on record . . ."

I hear a sob from my mother.

"For God's sake, Lori," Dad says.

"Shut up!" she screams. "Just shut up!"

Now I'm getting hysterical. "This isn't about you. It's about me. Can't you two just stop fighting for thirty seconds while I learn whether I'm gonna live or die?" I'm shaking, but I refuse to let them intimidate me. It's my life. I try to focus.

"Nicki," Dr. Graham continues, "we need to set your priorities. And, as I said, there are treatments . . ."

Dad interrupts. "We don't have to discuss this now, do we, Dr. Graham? She's had a terrible shock . . ."

I cut him off. "How long do I have, Doctor? I have to know."

He looks at me and we stare at each other.

"Tell me the truth, damn it. For once in my life, somebody tell me the truth." A kind of a fog envelops the room, smoky and dull. All the color suddenly drains out of everything for me. But whatever it is they have to say, I want to hear it. Now. Just drop the euphemisms.

The doctor looks at Dad and Mom and, one at a time, they each nod slowly. Why does he need their permission to talk to me? I'm the patient here. Me. A patient. How can that be? A minute ago, I was graduating. And now I'm a patient.

"Two to three months," says Dr. Graham.

I fall back onto the bed, as if somebody shoved me. Two to three months. Two to three months. Twotothreemonths. The words shock me like an electrical current. It's impossible to hear them or believe them. All I want to do is time-travel back to when none of this was true. Eliminate this entire time. Amputate it from my life.

This is how it is when you're given a death

sentence. Not that I ever wondered. I've wondered what a lot of things were like—being a
genius, for instance, or having a baby. I've always wondered what it was like to bungee
jump. To wear a bridal gown with a train. To
eat an entire cake. To own real jewelry. To see
the northern lights. To dance at dawn. To grow
old. There are lots of things I've wondered
about. Somehow, dying skipped the list.

Well, they've made a mistake. That much is
clear. I am not, repeat not, dying. I'm graduating. Working. Living. You don't do all those
things when you're dying. You don't die before
you reach legal age. This can't be true.

"Maybe you made a mistake," I say.

No response. So what? These people aren't
God. Doctors make mistakes all the time, don't
they? What is it Eric once said—fifty percent of
all doctors were in the bottom half of their class.
Maybe this doctor was in the bottom half.
Maybe he's wrong.

"I don't accept this diagnosis," I tell the group
surrounding my bed. "I don't even feel sick. It's
just a headache."

I hear Dad talking about experimental therapies. I hear Dr. Graham use words like "oncologist," "lobe," and "ultimately." The TV, bolted
to the wall, drones on, a soap opera. I hear it

through a speaker that's lying on my pillow. Who needs a soap opera? I'm living one. Or, more accurately, dying one. Emotions are racing through my body, aka the vessel of betrayal, like a flock of bats trapped in a too-small closet. Closing my eyes, I try to get a grip. Put yourself in my shoes, please. Now try to cry, or even feel, or even believe this is happening to you.

Once, I was cutting a watermelon front to back, and the knife moved faster than I thought and sliced through my thumb. I was cut to the bone, but, at first, I didn't even feel it. I just stared at my finger, laid open like a filet, and wondered what would happen next. But there's no script for this moment, or at least none that I will accept. Let's discuss the options here. Should I say a prayer, try to make a deal with God? Or just will it all to go away? My grandmother died of cancer. Basically, they took her away a piece at a time. She never left the hospital. The previews of my life, what's left of it, flicker before my eyes. Scene 1: hospital bed. Scene 2: chemo. Scene 3: hospital bed. Scene 4: treatment room. Scene 5: IV. Scene 6: hospital room. I don't want to go near the ending.

This has all the makings of a very, very bad movie. One I do not want to see. Here's what I think: the whole thing is ridiculous. I am not sick. These doctors are wrong, and if I stay here one more minute, they'll have me believing them. I have to get out before it's too late.

While the doctor is conferring with my parents, my body takes action on my behalf. It sits itself up, swings both legs over the side of the bed, and gets up. "I'm leaving," I announce. "I feel fine."

Everybody stops talking and stares for a second. Then they all scramble to stop me at once.

"Sweetheart!" My mother grabs my arm in a panic. "Please. We have to see the specialists. I know someone on the board at the University of Chicago. There's more tests . . ."

"To prove what? I've had enough. I'm out of here." I pick up my purse and walk toward the door. I don't feel frantic or crazed. Maybe when I get out of here, everything will be back to normal again. Please. Please. Please.

Mom and Dad are right behind me. "Nicki," Dad begs. "Listen to what the doctor has to say."

"Fine." I turn around and walk back to Dr. Graham.

"OK, Doctor, I'm listening. Can you cure me?"

"We need to sit down and go over the options, Nicki."

"Are there options?"

"There's a choice of protocols. Chemotherapy. Radiation . . ."

"Honey," Mom interrupts. "There are new treatments. We could go to Mayo Clinic . . ."

Dad suddenly looks wild. Upset or furious, it's hard to tell. "Get back in that bed, Nicki," he shouts.

"Back in the bed? Excuse me—who's this happening to?" I can't believe this. If these doctors are by some chance right, my parents expect me to go to my grave being treated like a child. And the worst part is, they may be right. I am a child. I've never had a chance to be out in the real world, never had anything but school and a dumb job waiting tables. And now, they're telling me to believe that I never will.

Mom turns on him in a fury. "This is not your decision, Dan. It's a family decision. For once, stop grandstanding."

Even now, they're at each other's throats. "Everybody out," I hear myself saying. "Clear the room. Now. I need to think!" Now I'm angry—furious, in fact.

"Honey . . ." Mom reaches out for me.

"Out!" It's a long, protracted scream. Startled, everybody actually leaves. "Close the door!" I yell after them.

Alone in the room, I have a talk with myself, which goes something like this: you can barely keep it together. You have to go on the assumption that this is a terrible, stupid mistake. A computer malfunction in a test. A mixed-up blood sample. Somebody else's CAT scan. A misdiagnosis. Medical incompetence. Then again, what if you are really sick? I know that this hospital is the last place I'd want to be, under any circumstances. I would never spend the time I have left in this place, on my back, staring at ceiling tiles and fluorescent lights, never seeing the sun. I feel any semblance of control I have crumbling, and I start to shout at anybody who could hear through the door. "I will not stay here, if it's the last thing I do!" Which obviously they think it will be.

"Who wants the pepperoni?"

The door bursts open. Eric has arrived, armed with three large pizza boxes. Emily has flowers, Tim has a wrapped gift of some sort, tied up with a pretty pink bow. They take one look at me and freeze.

"Oops," says Eric. "Maybe we should come back later."

"Nick?" says Tim, wondering.

They might as well hear it. "Supposedly, there is no later. This place sucks. I'm not going to stay here and be a victim of the system. Let's go." I leap off the bed and sweep out of the room, past my parents and the doctors, and down the hall. Tim runs up and puts his arm around me, but he looks at me like I am the madwoman I've become.

"Nicki, what is it? What's going on?" Tim asks, steadying me as I race down the hall. At this point, I can barely stand up. My knees are like water, my eyes a blur.

Mom rushes after us, and a few steps behind, I hear Dr. Graham tell Dad, "She's in denial. It's normal."

Normal for the bowels of Hades, maybe.

"What's going on here?" demands Emily.

"These idiots think I'm dying."

The ultimate stopper line. Followed by a frantic chorus of "What? What!"

"Don't joke," says Em. "It's not funny."

"Lori?" Tim turns to Mom.

She can't look at him.

We get as far as the lounge. Dr. Graham must have written me off as hopeless, because he's disappeared. My mother and father are still arguing in fierce whispers as they trail behind me. Mom wants me to go home with her. Dad wants me to move in with him. They both want me to go back into the hospital. Emily is smoking, even though it's not allowed. Tim has his arm around me, and Eric, aka Benedict Arnold, has sided with my parents and is trying to get me to go back to that goddamned hospital room, which he doesn't seem to understand is something I will never do.

"Can you believe this?" I gesture toward my parents, locked in their familiar, hostile face-off.

Tim shrugs. "They love you. Forget it. My God, this isn't real."

"Nick," says Eric, "the first rule in medicine is always get a second opinion. Even the doctors admit that. Of course there could be a mistake, or another point of view. You owe that much to all of us, and especially yourself. But you can't just write this thing off."

Emily nods. Her face is tear-stained, and black mascara has crept down her cheeks in two sooty trails. She looks like a candle in the process of melting. I put my arm around her. "It's a mistake," I say. "You'll see."

A nurse appears menacingly in the entrance to the lounge. "If you're going to smoke, you'll have to leave."

Emily dutifully mashes out her cigarette. The instant the white uniform exits the doorway, she lights another one. "A plan," she mutters. "We need a plan here." She wipes at her cheeks, smearing her makeup even more.

I lean into Tim. When I started at Northwestern, my family was shredded, but I found Tim, and now I can't imagine not being together. It was Tim who always knew I'd get into law school, who convinced me that I'd get the internship. We make an awesome team. We prioritized: it was all about our careers. He was going to be the big-time architect, and me, well, you know where I was headed. The internship was just the first step. Together, we were going to turn the world on edge. Now, instead, there's this. Tim, I plead silently, be my rock.

I can hear my parents.

Mom: "I'm taking a leave of absence immediately and Nicki will move in with me."

Dad: "Let's see what the oncologist says, Lori. We need information before we make any decisions."

Mom: "Didn't you hear what the doctor said, Dan? This isn't the time to distance yourself. Not this time, I won't allow it."

Dad: "Who's distancing? I just said . . ."

Anything is better than listening to this. I can't believe this—they're turning me into a pawn, treating me like I'm helpless.

"Stop it!" I yell. Dad breaks off, midsentence. Mom drops her purse, and keys and cosmetics spill onto the floor. They probably think I'm going to freak out. Let them. "Everybody," I announce, "this is a terrible mistake. Believe me. If

47

it will make you happy, set your mind at ease, I'll see another doctor, get another opinion at least, OK? But if the first opinion and the second opinion are the same, the third opinion gets to be mine."

"Good girl," Tim says, pulling me even closer. "You're going to be fine, Nicks. You'll see." He gives me the thumbs-up.

I hope to God he's right.

Chapter 4

My mother wrangled an extension on the lease, and Eric, Tim, and Emily went into power mode to try to get some answers and help me find the best doctors, treatments, and research. I did my part and checked into Northwestern Memorial for a week more, having more tests, going up to the University of Chicago, and consulting specialists, although I don't know why they call them that, since they had no special answers for me. They only had one answer, in fact, and it was always the same: the diagnosis was not a mistake. I have NF2.

Oh my God.

My mother tried to keep me there, in the hospital, tethered to the IV pole, but I put on my clothes and fled. The moment I realized that I was actually dying, I also realized that I would not spend one more second of my precious remaining life in the hospital.

Once, in an old black-and-white movie that was on TV at 3 A.M., I saw a re-creation of this war room where the Allies planned the D Day invasion. Except for Ike and Winston Churchill, as soon as I open the door to my apartment, I see pretty much the same thing right in my living room.

Tim is on line at the computer. Eric is on a phone with a headset. "It's imperative that I speak with Dr. Auerman in person, immediately," he's saying. "You don't understand . . ." Emily is on her cell. Stacks of papers, computer printouts, and medical textbooks cover every surface. There's a huge map taped to the wall, with major clinic cities throughout the world circled in red. Empty glasses, pizza boxes, and crumpled paper cover every surface. The flotsam of a siege.

Everybody freezes when I come in. Maybe they thought I was never going to leave the hospital. Ever. I don't want to talk to them. What do they know about what I am going through? What can anybody know? I go straight into my bedroom and keep going into the bathroom. I feel like throwing up. The door slams behind me.

The bathroom floor feels cool and comforting. I put my arms around my legs and pull my knees up to my body. This is the same bathroom I went into every day when I was normal, before this nightmare began. I would stand here in front of the mirror and try on lipstick colors, or brush my hair up into a clip, or check out which blouses went best with my interview suit. That was only two weeks ago. The bathroom's the same, but I'm not. Nothing's the same.

Now death is on the scene—my scene—in boldface. Everything else is, in an instant, nothing. The fact that I got a four point average and was class valedictorian is meaningless. What am I going to do with these accomplishments? Put them on my gravestone? NICOLE MCBAIN 4.0.

I wonder if I should just overdose on something right now, hoard toxic pills or pollute an IV. End it, like flicking out a light switch. At least I'd be in control. Is death better when you choose it than when it chooses you? Probably not. Death is never better. Life is better. That's what I want. Life.

Fact: I am, basically, dying. Zero prognosis. But what nobody knows is, I'm already dead. The Nicole they knew died back there in the hospital. I killed her, actually. She was weak, weak enough to get herself into this. I know that to survive, I have to be somebody I wasn't, somebody that can take it.

A knock on the door. "Nicki?" It's my mother. She was right behind me when I left the hospital. "I've called your father. He's coming right over."

"Go away. Just leave me alone." The headache is back, and the room swims. In my pocket are the pills they gave me at the hospital. I get up, pour a glass of water, and take two. What if I took three? Four? The whole bottle? The entire contents of the medicine cabinet? But then, that's the Old Nicki talking. My new and improved self will step in and take control.

Another knock. "Nicki?" This time, it's Tim.

"I'm busy. Just go away, all of you." I lock the door and stuff a towel under it. I'm crying again. Control? What control? I'm losing it. And why not? I'm going to die, and there's nothing I can do about it.

They say that when you are dying, your life flashes before your eyes. At least, that's what I read somewhere. But for me, it's the opposite. It's not my life that flashes in front of me, it's my lack of it. So much I haven't done. So much I thought I'd fit in later. So much planning, so little doing. So much to miss: love, marriage, giving birth, growing old, having fun, being free, just being. Science should come up with a package that has all those things in it so you can acquire them with one easy purchase: "The Life I Wish I'd Had."

Here's another fact: the bathroom floor is very uncomfortable, especially if you're in the fetal position, your head butting up against the toilet. If you're not going to kill yourself, you shouldn't hang out there. That's what I decide after an hour of lying on the floor and crying my guts out. What I'm doing here is, in a way, as revolting as dying. Wasting precious time. I force myself to get a grip. I'm not going to die right now, so I'd better pick an alternative I can live with. My New Self is going to win this one. She has to. She's all I have.

Get up. Get off the floor. Move yourself.

I come out of the bathroom, out of the bedroom, into the living room. Everyone looks at me with genuine fear. I feel powerful, my first glimpse at the power imminent death has on those around you. Everybody knows you have nothing to lose, so you could do anything. God knows what. I grab a handful of those papers. "What's all this?"

"We've been doing a little homework on NF2," says Em.

"I give you all an A." One pile at a time, I

dump the papers into the wastebasket.

Tim is right behind me. "What're you doing?" He starts to pull the papers out of the trash.

I grab them back and rip up as many as I can. "I get the third opinion, right?" At the computer, I read the writing on the screen. "Persons with NF2 frequently develop other sorts of tumors which grow on the coverings of the brain. These tumors can cause many kinds of neurological symptoms, depending on their location." I push the button. "Delete. Delete. Delete."

"Hey!" says Tim.

"That part of my life is over. Now, on to the rest."

"I've called Seattle, Nicki," says Dad.

"Good for you. No programs for me, though. No protocols. None of it. Tim, what's for dinner? I feel like a burger, fries, and a strawberry shake. With extra whipped cream. Now that's a plus— no need to worry about calories."

Tim looks at me warily. "Whatever you want, honey, but . . ."

"No buts. Everybody, I know how concerned you all are—Mom, Dad—I love you all. But I have to live the rest of my life. Live is the operative word here. I've been thinking about what I want to do next, and it has nothing to do with anything medical. You know, there are so

many things I haven't done. And I've decided—
I'm going to do as many of them as I can, while
I can."

"Nicki, you're under stress," Dad cuts in.

"Dad! Just this once, listen to me. I'm really
not going to have another chance, am I?"

What can he say?

"You know, I've worked so damned hard for
so many years, you guys. Double shifts at the
restaurant, double major at school. I know you
and Mom would have helped, but that was how
I wanted it. Then. Now I want a time with no
responsibilities, no tests, no pressure. Just some
time to see what a life of my own is like. It
doesn't look like I'll have another chance. Mom,
Dad, please, if you really love me, you'll help
me. Please."

I know they're going to fight about this, like
everything else. I know it's going to get ugly.
They're never going to stop trying to figure out
ways to cure me, or, at least, keep me alive.
They're going to keep calling specialists, doing
research, checking programs, protocols, statis-
tics. But I can see by their faces that they're also
going to do everything they can to make my
wish happen. Because they love me.

That night, Eric, Emily, Tim, and I go to
Barnes & Noble and clean out the travel section.

Atlases, maps, books on travel on $50 a day and travel on $500 a day—you name it, we bought it. Because this is the plan: we're going on a trip. I have no idea where. That's part of the adventure. Reckless abandon, that's my new thing. At least I feel like I'm alive again.

Back at the apartment, we put on the music and transform the former War Room into the Global Travel Agency.

"How about the Caribbean?" says Emily.

"Too tame," I say.

"Alaska?" says Tim.

"Too wild."

"Paris," Eric chips in.

"Too civilized."

"We're never gonna decide," says Emily.

She's right. And I have neither time nor patience for indecision. "We're going to decide this minute," I say. "An executive decision made by . . ." I pick a dart off a game on the back of one of the doors. "This dart. All in favor?" I don't give them time to answer. I just cover my eyes and hurl the dart at one of the maps that's on the wall. It lands in the middle of an ocean.

"Where's that?" I squint to see.

Tim pulls out the dart. "The Aegean Sea."

"That's it! A cruise of the Greek islands. Perfect. Fate has spoken." I should make decisions this way more often. Instantly I envision dancing with Tim on a moonlit deck, swimming in the warm island waters, touring ancient, ruined temples. It has to be a boat with sails.

"Nick, your parents said they were paying for everything, but I don't think they had this in mind. A cruise for all of us? To Greece?" Eric looks skeptical.

"Let's put it this way," I say. "They didn't use a cent of my college fund. This will be my education. Our education."

"In what?" asks Tim.

"All the subjects we missed in college. Fine wines, great food, romantic evenings, and nonstop partying."

Eric runs into the kitchen and reappears with a bottle of graduation champagne. He pops the cork. "To cruising!"

"Wait," I say, grabbing the bottle. "Before you pour that. You know, you guys, I know you all have plans. You don't have to put them off for me."

"I was taking off a month anyway," says Emily.

"I don't start school til September," says Eric. "Besides, we're all in this together, right?"

"Right," says Tim.

Emily holds up a gold card. "And I've got Daddy's card!"

"You sure?" What kind of friends are these, giving up their own lives to help you when yours is in trouble?

"We're here, wherever, whenever, however," says Eric.

I hug them all, then pour the champagne.

"There's just one critical thing," says Emily.

"What?" I ask. I'm a sloppy pourer. Champagne is bubbling over the rim of her glass.

"Bikinis. As in thong."

Sure enough, the next day, as soon as the stores open, we're there to try on thongs. Tim had to put in an appearance at the architects' office, but Emily and Eric are ready to rock. We booked the reservations over the internet—ten days on a gorgeous eight-hundred-foot windjammer called the Circe, two suites with all the extras. The suite I'll share with Emily even has its own private patio and a whirlpool tub. Done.

As I hold up the bits of material that pass for bathing suits, it's hard to believe that just two days ago I was lying immobilized in a coffin-esqe CAT scanner wondering if I'd ever get out of the hospital. And now here I am. I know I've made the right decision. And I feel fine. At least for now, and now is all that counts in this game.

"Do you think I can get away with this one?"

I wave a suit at Emily. "Tim's eyeballs will fall out of his skull."

"I still think he should have taken the day off," Em says, modeling a sun hat. "This is critical."

Eric shrugs. "Well, we know Tim. He has his priorities."

Emily gives him a look, but let's face it, Eric has never been a hundred percent for Tim, but that's because Eric's like your big brother. Nobody's good enough for his sister, right? I let the remark about Tim slide and take the hat from Emily. "I'm going to try them on together."

In the dressing room, I take a good look at myself. Five feet six, shiny hair, good skin, great figure, if I say so myself. The picture of health. Like a perfect peach that looks good on the outside, but when you bite into it, it's rotten under the skin. I pull off the bikini, put my jeans and T-shirt back on, and head back to the racks.

"Get up! She'll see you!" It's Eric. I can hear him across six racks of bikinis. But he doesn't see me. Emily is slumped against a mirror, crying. He's yanking her up by the arm. "Emily, for once, this is not about you. Nicki is our best friend, and she needs us."

Em's voice is muffled by the Kleenex she's got pressed to her nose. "How can she just go on like there's nothing wrong? I just don't get it."

"Look," Eric hisses. "She knows the score. She made a choice. And we're part of it. Whatever it takes, remember? You're her best girlfriend. Act like it! Don't you have any Visene? Quick!" He grabs a bathing suit and shoves Em toward the dressing rooms. That's when he sees me. "Em's just going to try this on. How'd yours fit?" He pushes her past me and into the dressing room.

Well, what did I expect? Did I just think they wouldn't notice I was dying, or they'd forget? It's hard on your friends, too, this dying thing. Maybe harder sometimes than on you. I follow them into the dressing room.

"OK, guys, we need to talk."

Em hangs her head. She doesn't want me to see how upset she is.

"I know how hard this must be for you both. But I don't know what I'd do without you. We really need each other now, but if you can't handle it, I wouldn't blame you."

Em finally looks at me. From the looks of her eyes, I guess she didn't have any Visene. "But, Nick, how do you do it? How do you act like everything's just the same—when it isn't?"

I put my arm around her. You know, when you've spent the last two weeks having people shovel pity on you, it feels pretty good to be the person comforting somebody else. "I know it's not the same, Em. But for just a little while, I want to feel like it is."

There's a banging on the door. "Men are not allowed in the dressing room!" a saleswoman admonishes.

"I'm not a man," Eric shouts back. "I'm their stylist."

We all fall apart laughing.

It's going to be OK.

That night, Tim takes me to the pier. It's one of my favorite places, because it has two of my favorite things—the lake and the Ferris wheel. At night, with all the lights and the lakefront skyline, it looks like a glittery party that a giant hand reached down from the sky and set down onto the surface of the water. Tim and I hold hands as we walk past the giant Ferris wheel, lit up like a Christmas tree five stories high in the sky, and past the cafes and crowds. Music floats through the air, and I can smell delicious things in layers in the air: the lake, and the food, and the slight fog that's rolling in, giving everything a soft edge and a glow. I like the way it feels so normal: if you'd look at us, all you'd see is two people on a date, strolling on the pier. Right now, there's something very special about normal. "It's going to be so great," I tell Tim. "This boat is incredible—it has a dozen sails, and we'll go to six different islands. Oh, be sure to get a mask and snorkel. You want one that fits. And you got your passport, right? Don't forget your passport."

Tim doesn't say anything. His mouth looks tight, like he's clamping it shut. I know that mouth.

"What? What is it?"

"Nick, I really need to talk with you. I'm having a really hard time with all this." He's looking at the ground.

"Well, so were Em and Eric. We talked about it and now it's OK."

"Well, I'm not OK. I just can't sit back and watch this and pretend." We stop walking. Tim stands there, his fists balled up at his sides.

"Who's pretending, Tim? This is as real as it gets."

Finally, he looks at me. "What if you need treatment on this trip?"

"I'll go home. Or maybe I'll die, and they'll bury me at sea, like a Viking."

"Shut up."

"So what are you saying?"

"I'm saying—I just can't go."

"What? It's all planned. We're leaving in three days! We've bought your ticket and everything. Are you really so scared to be with me?" I reach out to him, but he feels like cement.

"It's not you, Nick. There's a big project. My boss wants to put me on it—they told me today. It's the break I've been waiting for."

"Well, it's only ten days." Am I begging?

"Nick, I'm trying to be an architect. The end of the project is five years away." His voice is rational, as if he's trying to interject some sensibility into the issue.

I don't buy it.

"Right. Sorry, but I don't think I'll be there to see it." But I can't imagine seeing the Greek islands without Tim. It's hard to imagine doing anything without Tim, but I know that he has made some kind of decision, and I'm not part of it.

Tim puts his arms around me. "I feel so bad, Nick. I really wanted to go. You believe me, don't you?"

I stiffen. "Yeah, I believe you. Now just tell me the truth. I'm not into games right now. And I deserve the truth."

He sighs. "It's just too damn hard. I can't handle it. I can't believe this is happening to me."

To him. Him. I pull away. "I get it." I turn

around, start walking. Of course, Tim comes after me. I shake him off. "Don't. Just don't."

And I'm really not mad, because the worst
part is, I can't really blame him.

Chapter 5

*A*t O'Hare International Airport, we are standing at the gate, tickets and passports in hand, when my father makes his move. He, Kate, and Justin have joined my mom as the official send-off committee at the gate. Justin's pretty cute—he's made me a bon voyage card with crayons and colored paper. My mother is keeping a relatively stiff upper lip. We've already had a number of late-night discussions and sob sessions. She's resigned. And I cannot wait to get on that plane. It's not that I want to leave my parents so much as I need to find myself. Don't you think you should know who you are, as an independent person, before you die? Most people have several decades to figure this out. I've just got to speed up the process. When the plane leaves the ground, I'll leave all this behind and I'll pretend I'm going on a fabulous graduation trip with my best friends. Well, I am, aren't I?

Dad still isn't convinced. His teeth are clenched: the first clue. I can see the muscle in his jaw that sort of bobs around when he's upset. He pulls me aside and puts his hands on either side of my face. "I just got off the phone with Dr. Robert Charmichael. He's the leading man in NF2. He'll take you."

Mom is losing it. "Dan, did you forget? She's made her decision. We've promised to respect it."

He looks at her with a glance that says "She's committing suicide. Don't you care?"

She challenges with a look that says "More than anything. That's why I'm letting her go." Checkmate.

Ah, the beauty of those couples who have been a part of each other's lives—if not necessarily under the same roof—for many years. They can speak without saying a word.

Mom squares her shoulders and turns to me. "OK, sweetie. Just have a wonderful time. You've got your medicines. Eric has instructions from the doctors, and you have yours. You have your satellite cell phone. I'm just a call away. Everything should be fine."

Now, after all this, suddenly I feel like crying. "I promise to call from the boat, Mom. I love you."

Dad and I face each other. "I'm here if you need me, baby," he says quietly.

Everyone starts to tear up, when a booming voice breaks the mood: Eric is belting out the theme song from *Titanic*. "My heart will go o-o-on!" He winks and gallantly offers me his arm. "Let's go, Rose."

"More like the Unsinkable Molly Brown," I say, linking arms.

Emily takes my other arm, and we're actually off.

I love the name of our boat: *Circe*. Circe was a sorceress in Greek mythology, and I'm all for any kind of magic I can get at this point. The ship is gorgeous, white, sleek, and romantic. In other words, perfect. Eight hundred feet, four huge masts, sitting at the dock at Piraeus, which is the main port of Athens. The town itself is a hilly commercial peninsula, grimy and crowded with a gridlike plan of faceless apartment buildings—not exactly the low-key, picturesque scene we'd been expecting. High-rises, shipping offices, banks, and bumper-to-bumper traffic vie with the saturated blues of the sky and the sea.

There are no quaint cobblestone streets here. On the way to the quay, Eric has to dive sideways to avoid getting run over by a motorbike that jumps the curb to skirt a traffic jam. "Ah, paradise," he cracks. "It's changed a bit in the past three thousand years."

Emily waves her hand as we forge through the crowds to the boarding dock. She can't be bothered with banalities at a time like this: the girl has plans. She ticks off the highlights: "We're going to get massages right away. Manicures, pedicures. Then there's the Captain's Dinner tonight. That's when we can check everybody out." On board the ship, Emily has an instant footwear crisis, tottering on her four-inch Manolos.

"Welcome to the *Circe*," smiles a man in a white tailored uniform, who's obviously the captain. He's in his forties, isn't too tall, and has a Greek accent. At his side is a huge, burly guy whom he introduces as the first officer. Scurrying all around are the crew, gorgeous men in white shirts and black jeans.

Emily points to the crewman who is handling the ropes just ahead of us. "D'you think he's the masseur?"

I slide down my sunglasses and take a closer look. Great muscular build, about six-one, blondish-brown hair. OK, he's cute, but not my type. Or maybe I've been with Tim so long that I don't have a type anymore. At any rate, what's the point of thinking about romance? The prognosis in that area is what you might call fatally limited. "I'll stick with the Jacuzzi."

"Well, if you don't like him, there's more where he came from," Emily says, eyeing some of the other guys in the crew, particularly the first officer.

Just then, I manage to walk right into one of the ropes at the top of the gangplank, and my foot becomes caught.

"Excuse me, miss." British accent. The blonde crewman kneels down to disentangle my foot. "We don't usually tie up our passengers at the beginning of the cruise."

His fingers brush against my ankle and I feel myself blushing—something I never do. But there's something about the combination of the slightly sardonic smile and the accent that's disconcerting. I hop out of the rope, trying to look sophisticated and blase, as if I boarded major cruise ships all the time. "Thank you," I say. "I'm perfectly fine." I readjust my shoulder bag and catch up with Emily, who is being directed to our cabin.

The Jacuzzi, as anticipated, is not to be believed. Once we're in our suite, even before we unpack, I jump into bubbles up to my chin. We have a little sitting room with a sofa, TV, VCR, and CD player. There's a bar with an icemaker, and, in the wood-panelled bedroom, two double beds with crisp blue-and-white spreads beneath an overhead skylight. Huge glass doors slide open to our private patio and a spectacular ocean view.

Em sits on the edge of the tub and pours in half a bottle of champagne. "You've been soaking for an hour. I figured you could use a refill."

"I'm getting my sea legs. You know, I could get used to this."

"I've gone over the itinerary. Next stop is Mykonos." She unfurls a multi-panelled brochure. "Listen to this. It's all about the club scene. Then, for a side trip from Mykonos, we go retro. By like a million years. That's Delos. Incredible ruins. Then Ios, Santorini, Crete, Rhodes, Symi . . ."

I make a wet grab at the brochure. "Let me see that." There are pictures of the ruins interspersed with illustrations of the various gods and goddesses. "Hmm . . . according to this, the gods and goddesses loved their fun and games, especially activities held in their honor. So, I hereby dedicate this trip to Venus, goddess of love, and all those who have loved and will love." A knock on the outside door. "Get that, will you, Eric?"

He sticks his head in the bathroom and waves a huge bouquet of flowers. "FTD."

"See? It worked. I bet they're from Tim." Eric hands me the card. "Nope. From Dad, Kate, and Justin. So much for the goddess of love." I wad up the card and toss it across the room into the trash. Two points.

"Hurry up," says Emily. "You've gotta get out now. We don't want to miss leaving the dock. The brochure says it's a scene."

As the boat casts off, everyone is cheering and waving, and the band is playing Greek folk music. Confetti is flying, there's cheering and laughter. Emily and Eric are dancing with hand-kerchiefs, like Zorba. I move to the edge of the crowd, where it's quieter, and throw a rose from my flowers into the ship's wake. In a way, I'm sad to be leaving, because it means the trip is that much closer to being over.

We spend the rest of the day exploring the ship, then take our time getting dressed for the Captain's Dinner. "It's supposed to be casual," says Emily, "but after all, first impressions are first impressions." She's wearing a skirt so short that it barely fits the definition of clothing, a purple cut velvet tube top that shows her shoulder tattoo, and bracelets all the way up both arms. A magenta streak zigzags through her hair. Eric has on a T-shirt, vest, and skullcap.

In the lounge, everyone is mingling and indulging. The captain, along with the social director, stands at the entrance to the room, shaking hands. There is an appetizer buffet that could feed several indigent nations. We stake out territory at the bar, and Emily and Eric begin a running commentary on our shipmates. Before long, I'm on my third Belvedere martini, three olives up. Cheers.

Eric leans over. "Nick, take it easy. Are you supposed to drink with those medications?"

I shrug. Who reads the fine print? "I'm on vacation," I remind him. "Vacation from all that."

"You know, honey," interrupts a husky drawl, "I drank martinis at the Copa, I drank martinis at Harry's Bar in Venice, and at the Ritz in Paris." A woman swathed in a pink chiffon stole appears on the bar stool beside me. She gives me a lizard-lidded nod. Even if she hadn't started talking to me, I would have noticed her, with her tangerine-colored hair, jeweled cigarette holder, and long, dangly earrings. You might say she's the flamboyant type. "Take my word for it," she says conspiratorially, "these are the best. They go straight to your head." She toasts in my direction and drains her glass, then takes a long drag on her cigarette. "These first nights out are the best. You have the whole trip to look forward to. Kind of like when you're young—like you."

This makes me laugh, and the Pink Lady smiles.

Emily suddenly beckons. "We should go to our table."

"Not yet, I'm talking to my friend—"

"Shirley."

"My friend Shirley."

She waves her cigarette, wafting smoke. "You make so many new friends on a cruise. I met three of my ex-husbands on cruises. Two were widowers and one was a purser."

The phrase "three ex-husbands" catches Em's attention. "What's a purser?" she asks.

Shirley snorts, "Someone who cleans out your purse. But I'm a much better judge of character now, believe me. Take, for instance, him." She gestures to the man who is approaching us, camera at the ready. "I'll bet he has a fabulous character." Shirley leers lasciviously.

The man with the camera doesn't hear her and proceeds to introduce himself. "Excuse me, ladies. I'm Michael Schuster, the ship's photographer." A British accent—he's the guy with the ropes. In his tight black jeans and open-collar blue shirt, he's not bad looking. He's a little older than me, and he's got a certain sophistication about him that I'm not used to—definitely not the type you'd ever catch wearing a baseball cap, for instance. What I particularly notice, in spite of myself, are his hands. He has strong, beautiful, long-fingered hands that cradle his camera like a baby.

Emily narrows her eyes. "Didn't we see you manning the ropes? Or maybe it was swabbing the deck."

He's oblivious. Or maybe used to it. "We run a tight ship. Everybody does everything. In fact, the captain just cut my hair this afternoon." He smiles and lifts his camera. "Now, miss, would you mind if I took a shot of you for our new brochure?"

"You don't want my picture."

"But I do." He tinkers with the light meter. Those hands again. And this time, I notice his eyelashes, so long that they cast shadows on his cheeks. I force myself to stop noticing, but I wonder: if things weren't the way they are, would I let myself flirt with this guy? And because things are the way they are, I know that I can't. He probably thinks I'm a bitch, but that's

OK—better than him knowing the truth.

Shirley steps up, adjusting her stole. "You can take my picture anytime. I once posed for Herb Ritts."

The shutter clicks. "God," I whisper to Emily. "This is so Love Boat."

Now he's back to me. "Are you sure?"

"I'm—I'm really not in the mood," I stutter, surprising myself. "Why would you want a picture of me, anyway?"

He backs off, stepping away. "Well, I'm sorry. I sort of thought of it as a compliment."

"Of course it's a compliment," Emily cuts in. "My friend's still jet lagged. It was a long trip from Chicago. So where are you from?"

"New York," he says in his clipped voice.

Emily vamps, and he takes a few shots. The girl was born for the camera. "You don't sound like you're from New York," she points out.

"Actually, grew up in London, but I work in New York now, in the off-season."

"Great. Just two hours from Chicago!"

I have to put a stop to this. She's shameless. "Chicago is not two hours from New York, Emily."

"It is by plane."

Eric reappears with my refill. I grab it, down it a la Shirley, and use Eric as an excuse to get

75

away. "We're late for dinner," I announce.

As we're walking away, I hear Michael say to Emily, "What's her problem?"

Maybe I have a thing about somebody taking a picture of me that's going to be around longer than I am.

But Em says, "Nothing. She doesn't have a problem in the world."

The *Circe* has four dining rooms, but tonight's Captain's Dinner is in the Club Restaurant, which has brocaded chairs, peach-colored tablecloths, thick carpets, and little shaded lamps on each round table, like a cabaret. At one end of the room is a long table for ten, where the captain is sitting, flanked by Shirley, who has wasted no time schmoozing him up. Eric, Emily, and I are seated with the first officer, whose name is George, much to Emily's pleasure.

Across the room, by a banquette, I notice the photographer, Michael, working the room, taking pictures of the tables. The room is dimly lit, but I think I catch him glancing at me. Or maybe not—it's hard to tell in this light. At any rate, he probably thinks I'm strange, since nobody else is refusing to have their picture taken. Maybe I've become a challenge, the one subject he can't capture.

I focus on my langoustine appetizer and suddenly, he's behind my chair. I don't see him, but somehow I know it.

"Michael, here, take one of George and me!" Emily calls out as she spots him.

He touches my shoulder lightly. "Don't worry. You won't be in the shot. I'm shooting over your shoulder."

I sip my champagne and don't turn around, trying to ignore him. He is definitely a pest.

Emily gets up to dance with George, and Michael leans on the back of her seat. "You know, there used to be primitive people who never wanted anyone to take their picture because they felt the image on paper stole their soul. Are you one of those people?"

"I don't think I'm primitive. I have a microwave. Photography just seems so narcissistic to me."

"The photographer or the subject?"

"The subject, of course. Who wants to look at their picture?"

He laughs. "Well, that's a relief. For a minute there, I took it personally."

Then he's gone.

The next morning, we make our first trip ashore, to a beach that is called Super-Paradise. As we skirt the harbor, I soak in the view. The blazingly whitewashed, clay-roofed buildings of Mykonos look to me like they're made of sugar cubes, trimmed in bright blue woodwork and stacked along the hillside, with a jumble of brightly colored boats bobbing in the harbor. On a hill beyond the harbor there's a lineup of windmills standing in a row. It's beautiful but not idyllic or quaint—this is clearly a busy port, although it bears no resemblance to the kind of steel-and-concrete business I'm used to seeing at home. When we reach the beach, we climb off the water taxi ladder into the shallow, warm water, and Michael is right there on shore, taking everybody's picture. Except mine. I guess he got the hint last night.

Emily vogues on the beach, and he heads in our direction.

"Maybe you should've been a model," says Eric.

Em waves with her hat. "Hi, Michael!"

But he heads past Emily to me. "I'm really sorry about last night," he says. "I didn't mean to upset you by being too pushy about the pictures." In his bathing suit he looks tan and muscular, the kind of body that comes from doing real work, not working out in a gym in front of a mirror.

Emily, protective girl that she is, answers for

me. "Sometimes she doesn't feel very social, OK?"

Obviously, there's no avoiding this guy. "Don't make excuses for me, Em. Sometimes I don't feel very social, that's all."

"I know what you mean. Sometimes I don't either. That's why I stay behind this." He holds up his camera.

Emily looks at Michael, then back at me, then at Eric.

"Ahem—I see an ice cream vendor. Let's go," says Eric, dragging Emily off with him. "See you at the beach, Nick." They're not too obvious.

"Are all these pictures for the brochure?" I ask Michael. We're standing inches apart, practically naked. Suddenly I wonder if my bikini is too revealing. I pull up the top a quarter of an inch.

"Actually, I'm on my break," he says. "I'm trying to put together a portfolio. There's a Soho gallery that's always introducing new photographers."

"Are they showing your work?"

We're walking toward the beach, and the scene ahead is wild, even at this range. Club music is blasting from the beachfront bars. We pass a complete cross section of humanity, every sort of people imaginable: gay, straight, pierced, tattooed, shaved, you name it. Michael starts firing off shots of some of the weirder characters.

"I don't know if I'm any good yet," Michael says as he focuses.

"But you'll never know if you don't get out there."

He smiles over the top of the camera. "Well, if I ever have a show, you'll have to come." Funny, I hadn't noticed that he has a dimple on one side—just one side.

"Sorry," I mumble. "I don't think I'll be able to make it."

Now Michael drops the camera and lets it dangle around his neck. "Wait a minute. How do you know?"

"Some things you just know."

"Such as?"

I try to switch the subject. "There's something people who use cameras as shields don't want you to know."

He reaches into his camera bag and hands me a bottle of sunblock. "You might want to use this. The sun gets pretty intense."

He's good—turning the tables so smoothly that I wouldn't have noticed if I hadn't just done the same thing. I call him on it. "You're changing the subject. We were talking about you."

"What do you think I'm hiding? I'm just a guy with a camera."

"Everybody's hiding something. Even from themselves, sometimes."

Two topless girls stroll by. Michael raises his eyebrows behind his sunglasses. "They're not hiding much."

I can't help it. I start laughing—the first real laugh I've had in weeks. "OK," I concede. "You don't have to tell me your secrets, because I'm not going to tell you mine."

"Fair enough." He says it like a challenge. But I will never let him know what's really going on with me. I guess I don't mind it if he takes my picture or talks to me. I would, on the other hand, mind it very much if he felt sorry for me.

He plucks the sunblock out of my hand. "I can see you're the stubborn sort." He pours some lotion into his hand and rubs it on my arm. "You're getting burned."

Emily and Eric are just ahead of us. I trot ahead to catch up. It feels great to be out here, running on the hot, white sand. The last few weeks never happened. I will them away forever.

"So did we miss anything?" asks Eric.

I turn back to Michael. "Michael's doing sunblock applications."

Emily drops her strap. "I think I'm getting burned right here, Michael," she calls over her shoulder, stroking her chest.

He catches up and peers at her chest. "Yeah, right you are. Watch out for blisters. Here you go." He tosses her the sunblock bottle.

Em leans over and whispers to me, "That's it. He passed the acid test. If a man is standing next to you and me and he ignores my chest like that, it can only mean one thing: he's gotta be totally into you."

My cheeks are burning. Am I blushing, or am I sunburned? Luckily the music is blaring so loud that I don't think Michael heard. I start to allow myself the luxury of feeling normal, of pretending nothing is different about me than any other young woman who might or might not have a man interested in her, but it doesn't last. I remember Tim and his reaction. How would a total stranger feel about me if he knew? Whether Michael likes me or doesn't like me, whether anybody in the world does, for that matter, means absolutely nothing. With me, the outcome will always be the same: a dead end. OK, it's a bad pun, but it's the truth, isn't it? Suddenly the beach feels very cold, and I turn around and run through the crowd to the water's edge.

For a minute, I just stand there, taking deep breaths. The Aegean laps at my ankles, a kitten of an ocean, soft and warm. I go in to my knees, then dive in headfirst and start swimming. It's been a while since I swam any distances, but I stroke and kick and stroke and kick, my face in the water, salt stinging my eyes. I have no idea where I'm headed. I swim past the other swimmers and some small boats. The horizon looks welcoming. I head there. Out to sea. I'm weightless in the salt water, as if I'm in a gigantic womb. A wave washes over my head and I gulp a mouthful of water. Coughing, I finally turn and see the shore, which seems blurry and very far away. How far have I gone? I'm tired now, I'm choking. What if I can't make it back?

I close my eyes and let myself go limp, hoping to sink.

If I die here, like this, maybe it's for the best. I breathe in more water and gag. Part of me just wants to let go, give in.

But there's another part of me that, in spite of everything, resists. I lift my head and calculate the job ahead, but I'm sure I can never make it to shore. I've even swum too far away from the small boats for anyone to see me. Emily and Eric probably think I just took a walk on the beach. Flailing in the water, I'm struggling against myself as much as the sea.

Suddenly, out of nowhere, a hand grabs my bikini top and holds me firmly at the surface.

I'm pulled up into a boat and onto a Sunfish. My bikini top snaps as I flop onto the Sunfish, and I'm gasping for breath and coughing up seawater, but I'm safe.

It's Michael.

He leans over and thumps me on the back. "Are you crazy?" he yells. "There's current out here. You could be carried right out to sea!"

Tell me about it. I sit up shakily, hacking, catching my breath, but then I realize I have no top and cross my arms over my chest.

"Don't worry about it, it's a topless beach." Michael pulls in the sail, turns the tiller, and we come about and head back to shore, the little boat skipping over the waves. "Are you OK?" Michael yells over the wind.

I nod. Yes, I'm OK Ladies and gentlemen, the soap opera is over. I had my chance to take a shortcut, and I opted for the long way around.

"I looked up and saw you heading out. I had my telephoto lens, and I could see you were headed for trouble, so I borrowed this boat. You can't swim alone like that. It's dangerous."

"I'll try to be more careful."

In the shallow water, Michael drops the line and lets the sail go loose, and the boat stops. He helps me stand up; my legs are rubbery. I wade weakly to shore as he beaches the boat.

Emily runs over. "Did you guys go sailing? I'm jealous." Clueless, she zeros in on my bare chest. "Going native?"

"I lost it in the water."

"Well, that's one way to make friends."

I start to shiver, and she rummages in her oversized straw beach bag and hands me a T-shirt. I slip it on over my thong bottom.

"I'm going to find Eric. You OK?"

I nod, and Emily trots off down the beach. Michael hands me a Coke. "Here, wash down some of that salt water." He's giving me a very intense look.

"I'm fine," I insist. "Thank you for coming out for me. I was getting tired."

Michael dries himself off, and Emily pulls his camera out of her bag and hands it back to him. It's all so normal. Nobody knows what almost happened.

An old woman, incongruous in a black dress, walks by holding a worn basket.

"See how she contrasts with the people all around her?" Michael asks as he focuses his camera. "She's so classic and timeless, and they're so modern and crazy. That's what will make the shot interesting." The shutter clicks and his film whirrs forward.

"You're an artist, so why did you come on this boat?" I ask.

Michael shrugs. "I had to get away," he says. "Things weren't going so great for me at home, and my father was pressuring me to go into the family business."

"Which is?"

"Sausages."

"Oh. Somehow I don't see you with sausages for the rest of your life."

"Neither did I. But my father, well, he didn't think I could ever make it as a photographer." His voice takes on an edge. "There were words between us. So I answered an ad and took this job. I made a deal with the captain—if I took the pictures the cruise line wanted, he'd let me take the pictures I wanted. I got away, I got to travel, take pictures, and think about what I wanted to do."

"That's sort of why I'm here, too."

"You're getting away from something?"

"You might say that."

"What might that be?"

"A secret."

"A woman of mystery. Maybe you'll share that secret with me. You know, I know there's something going on with you. I followed you to the water because, back there on the beach, you seemed totally upset, like the world was coming to an end. I saw it in your face. Why did you swim out there like that? You don't seem like the reckless type. You're not coming clean, are you, Nicole?"

"I just got in a bit over my head."

Michael checks his watch. "You certainly did. And that's it?"

"That's it."

He shakes his head. "Well, I have to get back to the ship. My shift is coming up. Once you've dried out, you should think about going into town for the clubs tonight. It's fun. It'll cheer you up." Again, that intense look; he sees through me.

"The clubs?" I sense that with Michael, fun would only be the start of something I'm in no position to deal with.

"The most amazing club is Pierro's. I'm going to be there after dinner, taking pictures. Maybe I'll see you?"

"Maybe." We stand there, looking at each other. He's waiting for me to respond, play the game. "Thanks again for the boat ride."

"Well, if you decide to drop by, I'll be the one with the camera." He smiles, but he's clearly confused about me. Why not? I'm not making any sense, unless you're wearing a lab coat and you've taken a peek at my CAT scans recently. As Michael walks back across the beach toward the water taxi, I watch his footprints in the sand. After a minute, they are washed away by the waves, and when I look up, he's gone.

Chapter 6

My better judgment tells me to avoid Pierro's. There must be other places to party, places where I won't torment myself by running into Michael. It's pretty clear to me that if I see much more of him, I'm going to have to start explaining things, and that would be a disaster. But the combination of Emily, Eric, and Shirley is like a force of nature, and it's either go with them or spend the evening alone on the ship, and I certainly didn't come all the way to Greece to sit alone in my cabin, Jacuzzi or no Jacuzzi. Shirley has been to Pierro's before and, according to her, it's a major scene, a not-to-be-missed attraction that's right up there with the Parthenon. "Of course, there are some other hot spots," she says. "The Windmill Disco, a few others—they tend to change year to year. But I like Pierro's. It's on the main drag and caters to the beau monde."

If you say so, Shirley.

Emily has gone all-out Goth for the occasion: long black skirt, slit to the hip, combined with a baby T that shows her pierced navel, and a collection of crosses clanging from chains around her neck. Her hair is in braids, courtesy of Eric. I've got on a short white dress, my hair slicked back. With my new tan, I look pretty good—at least on the outside. When I look at myself in the mirror, it doesn't seem possible that the inside of my head is on a suicide mission. One good thing: the headaches are under control, thanks to the steroids and medicine cocktails, and I like to let myself think that maybe, just maybe, I might get over this thing.

So, fine. Pierro's it is.

The town is a maze of crowded streets. There's a ban on cars, and after dark the place is one big party—music blasting from dozens of clubs along the harbor and up the hill, people swarming noisily through the streets. But Pierro's is the most crowded place of all. I can't even squeeze inside, so I sit with Emily at a little cafe across the street, where I can watch the action through the big floor-to-ceiling windows. Somehow Shirley and Eric make it not only inside but to the front of the room, where they are dancing on a mammoth speaker. Across the room from them is a drag queen dressed like Marie Antoinette, dancing on another speaker in an outfit that includes a period brocade gown and a foot-high powdered wig topped by a bird-cage.

Emily gives me a nudge. "Look who's here."

Michael is coming out of the club with his camera. He spots us and maneuvers through the mob of people in front of the club to our table. He's in a blue cotton shirt, with the sleeves rolled up, and denim shorts. He has great legs, and when I see him, I instantly forget that I didn't want to run into him tonight.

"I got a great shot of Marie Antoinette," he says excitedly.

"For the boat brochure?" I ask.

"No, I took Shirley's picture for that," he laughs. "She was only too happy to oblige. No, Marie Antoinette is for my private collection."

Eric appears at the table, soaking wet. "Shirley got asked to dance by a count. So Emily, you're up." He grabs her by the hand and drags her off into the crowd, leaving me with Michael.

"So," I say, "are you still on your shift?"

He checks his watch. "It's over in three minutes, but I'm thinking of quitting early. Want to go on a little side trip?"

"Where?"

"Someplace very exclusive."

Can I tell you something? All of a sudden it does not matter to me where we go, because at this moment it feels totally right to be going anywhere, anywhere at all, with Michael. Am I being indulgent? Maybe so, given the circumstances. But, I convince myself, I have to lighten up. After all, what harm is there in having a nice time with a person you obviously click with? And wasn't that why I decided to come to Greece—to indulge myself?

We make our way through the mob scene, and Michael has to hold my hand so we don't get separated as we pass dozens of bars, each with a crushing mob scene. I'm glad Michael's in the lead, because this is a place where you could get lost in a hurry. The streets seem like a maze, winding and cramped. There are no cars, just people and the occasional cat brushing my legs as it slinks defensively through the crowd.

"How do you find your way around here?" I ask as we round yet another confusing turn. The town is not unlike a labyrinth.

Michael laughs. "They laid the town out like this in ancient times on purpose. To protect them from pirates. The Cyclades used to be a major stopoff for pirates. I guess they figured that if they confused them enough, they'd go away. The buildings used to be painted dark back then, too, so they didn't stand out and attract attention when the pirates sailed by."

As we approach the harbor, dozens of boats of all sizes sport strings of festive lights of their own. The crowd thins out as we walk over a small hill, and finally we come to a high seawall where waves are crashing into the rocks.

"So where are we going?" I ask.

Michael stops. "Right here. The dance floor is much less crowded here." He clamors up the seawall, reaches down for me, and pulls me up with him.

The music in the distance is muffled by the sounds of the sea, but songs drift around us as if the notes were floating, suspended from the stars. Michael holds out his arms in an invitation to dance.

"I don't think you're going to be needing this." I slip his camera over his head and put it on a ledge. "So what're you going to do without your shield?"

"I guess I'll be defenseless, won't I?" he laughs.

I step close and we begin to dance. "Good," I say. "Then we're even."

I step into his arms, and we dance slowly. My head finds its way onto his shoulder, I feel his heart beating, his hand pressing the small of my back, and I am suddenly very glad that Tim didn't come on this trip. It's strange how, after all the years Tim and I were together, being with Michael, feeling him close like this, feels even more natural. But then, I tell myself, maybe he's had practice. "So do you take all the girls out here?"

"No," he says into my hair. "No girls. Just one woman."

Woman. To be thought of as a woman, the one thing that every girl takes for granted that she'll be, and that I thought I'd never have a chance to become. Our faces are so close I can feel his breath, and he must be able to feel mine. I close my eyes and try to relax and, somehow, I do.

But I can't help it, I feel something new. Tell me if I'm crazy. Here I am, in a country and a city I've never been in before, in the arms of a man I barely know, and I feel like I've come home, like I belong right here, right now. With him.

The night surrounds us, and there's no doubt it's a romantic setting. I almost don't want to breathe, in case that would disturb the perfect balance of the moment. We're like two magnets. Somewhere there are sides of us that are magnetically attracted, but we're presenting the opposite poles to each other, the sides that hold each other off—but you know that with the slightest tilt, the tiniest shift in the balance of things, everything would be different.

Michael leans into me and gives me the softest, most gentle kiss, like petals. It's very chaste, in a way—totally respectful, almost old-fashioned, as if he's asking permission for something more that we both know is coming. No boundaries are crossed.

But, somehow, they all are.

We catch the last water taxi back to the ship, and I let myself into the suite as quietly as I can. It doesn't matter. At the first sound of the key in the door, Emily is awake in the bedroom and bolt upright in bed.

"My God," she says groggily, "I was starting to get worried. You disappeared."

"Shh—go back to sleep. I'm just here to get my sneakers. I'm going to the crow's nest."

"What the hell is the crow's nest?"

"I'm not sure—but I'm meeting Michael there."

Now she's really wide awake.

95

"What!!"

I'm out the door, sneakers in hand. How many heartbeats does it take to get to the crow's nest? I think my heart is asking that question, because it's beating much faster than usual as I make my way up the mast with Michael. His hand is at the small of my back, the wind is whipping my hair like the whitecaps far below. "How high are we?" I venture to ask.

"Three or four feet. Step now, step, step."

We inch upward.

"Three or four hundred feet, you mean."

"Well, I didn't want to take you up here. It's totally against the rules. It was you who insisted. But we're almost there. Just don't look down. And whatever you do, don't fall. I could get into a lot of trouble if you did something like that and they found out I took you up here."

We make it to the crow's nest and I stand, gripping the sides, circled by Michael's arms. I've never felt so safe.

"This is the most peaceful place on earth," he says.

"It's perfect." You can see the lights of the entire harbor and town spread out like a bag of jewels spilled on the hillside. I feel like I was meant to be here at this moment with Michael, like it was all supposed to happen, getting on this boat, going to Greece, that dart finding its way to the map where it did.

"You're not afraid, are you?" Michael asks.

I think back to the hospital and the IV and the CAT scan machine and the charts and the doctors' hopeless faces. What is there to be afraid of after that? "No way."

"Well," he says, "I'm afraid."

"Of what?"

"Us. You and me. This is all moving too fast."

"You don't understand," I correct him. "It's actually not moving fast enough."

"Nicki, we have all the time in the world."

I should tell him. But if I do, then what? What would be the point? I remember the look on Tim's face. No, I will not tell Michael. Not ever.

I feel his lips on my hair, and I turn into him. The kiss that happens isn't soft and sweet. No Hallmark card. It's more like a collision, one that couldn't be avoided. We kiss and hold each other for a long time, and it's just Michael, me, and the stars.

"Is this OK?" Michael says, his voice soft.

I can only nod, because it's both OK and not OK. I'm fooling myself and this man, and he's the only one of us who doesn't know it. I know that's not fair to either of us, but I seem to be totally unable to stop myself from wanting to be with him, hold him, fall in love with him. It's irrational and perfect. Thrilling and awful. Wonderful and terrible. But I want it more than I've ever wanted anything. There's nothing to do but let it happen.

When I open my eyes, time has skimmed off what's left of the night, the sky has a glow, and it's almost dawn. I wish I could stop the sun from coming up. I wish time would stop and there would never be another day.

"Young lady," Michael says, "we have to get you down." His arms are around me, and neither of us makes a move. "The crew will be out on deck any minute, and you are not supposed to be up here."

As he says this, a white-uniformed figure crosses the deck. "It's George, doing the morning checklist."

George disappears back inside the boat and we make our way back to the deck. On the way down, I'm not scared of heights at all. Or of anything.

The next morning, Emily has to drag me out of bed to make the boat for Delos. We take the shuttle into the harbor at Mykonos, and from there, it's a forty-minute ferry ride to Delos.

"I can't believe you almost slept through

this," says Emily once we're on the ferry. "Delos! This was one of the most sacred places in ancient Greece. The entire island is a living archaeological museum, for God's sake. It's supposed to be incredible." She thrusts her guidebook at me. "Read."

I have to admit, I'm still in a cloud from last night. The whole evening was like a dream. Did it really happen?

Emily eyes me. "So what happened last night?" She pokes Eric. "I was up all night, I was so worried. She didn't come in till it was light out."

"My, my, my." Eric lifts his eyebrows. "So did you sleep with him?"

"No! He was a total gentleman."

"So he's gay," declares Eric.

"Definitely not," I say, whacking Eric with the guidebook. "Unfortunately for you! And do I really have to discuss my sex life on a boat full of people? Get your minds out of the gutter!"

"Enquiring minds want to know," says Eric.

"Well, if you insist, we went to the crow's nest."

"What the hell is the crow's nest?" Emily is now totally exasperated.

"I think it's the place where I fell in love."

"What! Love! Details, I need details!"

"There are none." I start calmly reading the guidebook.

Em makes a grab for it. "You can't read that at a time like this!"

I swivel in my seat and evade her grasp. "Oh yes I can. Hmm. It says here that in 426 B.C., the Athenians issued an edict forbidding all births and deaths on the island of Delos." I slam the book shut and hand it back to Emily. "Perfect. I'll just never leave Delos. End of problem."

"Good thinking," says Em.

The ferry is docking now, and everybody is scrambling to their feet. Em grabs my arm. "You have to tell us everything."

"What's this about falling in love?" Eric demands.

"I wish I could explain it, but I can't."

"You could try," Emily insists.

"Let me figure it out first, OK?" The truth is, although I've always shared everything with Eric and Emily, my feelings about Michael are something I want to keep private, at least for now. It's all so new, and so different from the way I felt about Tim when I met him, or even at the height of our relationship. Tim was one of our crowd, someone that fit in with my life, a boyfriend. Michael is none of the above. The question is, what is he? And what, if anything, am I to him?

We disembark from the ferry, siphon through the ticket kiosk, and spend the next three hours exploring the sights. The first place we visit is a market where the bases of the monuments built by guildsmen thousands of years ago are still standing. Emily immediately falls in love with the Terrace of the Lions, where five of an original sixteen ancient, weather-beaten stone statues of lions stand guard.

"The ancient Greeks knew how to treat animals," she announces respectfully as we take each others' pictures with the lion statues. "They worshiped them."

From there, we move on to the Sacred Lake and, finally, some excavations of mansions. Eric's favorite: The House of the Comedians. Finally, we see the remains of a theater that once sat more than five thousand people. It's unbelievable that so much history could be crammed into one small island, that so long ago, this jumble of ruins was so alive, and now it's just a part of history. Thinking about this, I don't feel much like talking. I'm simply soaking it all in. For the first time since the hospital, I feel like my life is falling into some sort of perspective. I don't feel so singled out.

The thing that's clear now is that there's a pattern—everything has its time, and then it's gone, and there's no stopping this endless cycle, no matter who you are. I can't, and neither could the five thousand people who were once in that theater. The ancient Greeks dealt with the inevitable by creating rituals and gods. They were lucky, in a way. We have to figure things out for ourselves.

The next time I have a chance to see Michael is at lunch, which is a buffet on the *Circe*'s promenade deck. Greek folk music is playing, and most people are in bathing suits or shorts. Shirley grabs Eric and starts showing him how to do a dance with a napkin. The captain, George, and the officers are circling through the group, and the captain comes up to me. "Are you ladies enjoying your trip?" he asks, flashing a white smile, which Eric is sure is laminates. The guy looks like he came from Central Casting. He checks out Emily through his aviator-style tinted glasses.

"It's great," I say.

"And you have sampled our Greek specialties? We have the best moussaka in the islands on this boat."

"Oh yes," says Emily, who eats only salads, "I adore moussaka." Maybe she thinks it's a kind of Greek lettuce.

"Today there will be a program after lunch on the *Odyssey*. We are revisiting some of the places in the story on this trip. You might find it enjoyable."

"I wouldn't miss it," says Emily.

"And when you go sight-seeing, ladies, I suggest you be careful. Young women like you need to exercise caution, unfortunately, especially in dealing with the men you may encounter." He stares directly at me, and I know he knows I was up in the crow's nest.

The captain moves on among the guests, and I catch up with Michael.

"Hi."

He doesn't turn his head. "I'm working," he says as he changes lenses.

"So when can we talk?"

"I don't know." He walks away from me to shoot a platter of fruit.

"Is something wrong?" Something is definitely wrong. I know I'm more appealing than a sliced mango.

"No. I just have to work." He buries his face in the camera and starts shooting. The shield is back.

"For God's sake, Michael, is this some sort of game? Because if it is, I don't want to play."

"I just can't talk," he says.

"Michael!" the captain barks, and Michael turns abruptly away.

"What's with him?" asks Emily.

"Who knows? Something."

"Well, I guess."

I follow him out of the lounge, into a passageway. It's narrow, and our bodies almost touch. "So?" I demand.

His face tightens. "Listen, Nicki, if I talk to you I'm taking a big risk."

"So am I. I don't want to want to talk to you, you know. I came on this trip to have fun, to forget about everything in my life, to not be stressed out."

Michael rubs his forehead. "Look, Nicki. My job is on the line. The captain practically keel-hauled me."

So. "I know he saw us. That's not good, huh?"

"No. Not good. The crew is not supposed to—how'd he put it?—'fraternize' with the passengers."

" 'Fraternize'? That's what we were doing?"

We both laugh. Then we're quiet.

"So I won't see you?" I've never felt so empty. But it wouldn't be right to make Michael put his job on the line. What's the trade-off here? A few nights with a woman he'll never see again or his career? "I understand," I whisper.

*   *   *

The next day, the boat takes us to Ios. "You're going to love this place," says Emily, who has assumed the role of our resident tour guide. "It's the party island."

I decide to forget about Michael and have a good time in spite of myself. We disembark—I'm picking up a maritime vocabulary—at the port of Gialos, with its requisite combination of picturesque white buildings and churches and noisy waterside bars and discos, and catch the cruise line's private shuttle bus to the village.

"So fill us in," says Eric as the bus winds its way up the hill.

"Nothing to say."

"Come on," says Emily.

"Well, there's nothing. The captain won't let the crew associate with the passengers. Michael could lose his job. But it's cool. It wasn't going anywhere."

"That's not how it looked to me," mutters Emily.

"So does Captain Bligh have to know every little thing?" says Eric.

"There's always Tim," jibes Em.

"Listen, there is no way I am going to get involved. I just want to have a good time, remember?"

Emily looks uncomfortable. I put my arm around her. "It's OK, Em. You have to laugh about these things. I had a good time with Michael. That's all that counts. Nothing's forever. It was no big deal."

"You sure?"

I nod decisively. "Right. No big deal."

On Ios we discover that the day's excursion is a sight-seeing trip to Homer's grave. I check the guidebook. "Supposedly Ios is the place that Homer chose to return to die. Perfect." I slam the book shut. Is it any surprise that I don't want to visit a grave?

"I've already seen it ten times," says Shirley, with a wave of a jewelled cigarette holder. "They don't even know for sure that it's him in there. Let's have some fun instead." So Emily, Eric, and I join Shirley exploring her favorite tavernas on Ios, starting with a lunch of grilled sardines and wine, and then moving on to the next taverna for ouzo, and then the next. I don't think I'm drinking that much, but, by taverna number three, it hits me.

"Ooh, my young friend, we are cutting you off!" chides Shirley as she grabs my glass.

"Stop right there!" I slap her hand. "No fraternizing! No fraternizing with the passengers!" I think I'm yelling. "Did you people hear me . . ."

"We're out of here," I hear Emily say. She and Eric swoop in and pull me to my feet, which is a good thing, since my legs won't work. Net result: Eric has to practically carry me back to the launch. I spend the trip back to the *Circe* leaning over the side, completely wasted.

As Eric and Emily are hauling me out of the launch and trying to get me to stand on my own two feet on the deck, who should emerge but Michael.

"Go ahead! Take my picture, then!" I say furiously to him, my knees buckling. "Here's Nicole, crawling back to the boat. What a pretty picture!"

Emily tugs my arm and pushes me past Michael, but I turn my head and yell over my shoulder, "Maybe you'll want this one for the brochure!"

Then I throw up.

Chapter 7

"*O*h my God," I moan. "Did I make a total ass of myself in front of everybody?" I can't remember the last time I actually got myself drunk. Losing control like that is definitely not my style. I'm not sure whether to blame my current misery on prolonged jet lag, ouzo, my medicines, or myself. On the bright side, however, I know my pounding headache is due to something other than my condition.

"Define 'everybody,' " says Eric. "If you mean everybody as in *everybody*, no. If you mean everybody as in *somebody*, yes."

I wish I could just sit on this hill and enjoy my lunch, but I feel completely wiped out. "It's Shirley's fault," I say.

"Yeah, that's the ticket—blame Shirley," says Eric.

"Nick, don't worry, Michael didn't notice a thing," says Emily defensively, shooting Eric a withering look.

"I could care less what Michael thinks, you guys."

"Whatever," shrugs Eric.

Last night the *Circe* sailed to Santorini. From the terrace of the Atlantis Hotel, where we're having lunch, there's a sharp contrast where the cobalt blue of the ocean meets the white buildings of the hillside, with their flat and domed roofs, all of which seem to tumble down the steep hillside to an abrupt end at the water's edge. The buildings here are so white that they seem to have been bleached, and the entire town seems to be carved into or set on thousand-foot-high volcanic cliffs, which are scruffy, dry, treeless, and terra-cotta red. It's when you're actually on the island, looking out to sea, that you're the most taken in by these views, which are both endless and spectacular. Every turn of your head offers another postcard-perfect snapshot: the Aegean, the cascades of brilliant bougainvillea and geraniums, lava-stone walls, church domes as blue as the sky and the sea. I know I should be absorbing the scenery, but all I can see is a memory of Michael's face.

Eric nudges me as we leave the hotel for a

tour of the island. "So, Nick, you need a Tylenol?"

"What?"

"You're not yourself."

I realize that I'm walking aimlessly down the black cobblestone paths. This is not like me, always purposeful, agenda-driven, and directed. But, of course, I'm not me anymore, am I?

Suddenly a motorcycle weaves through the crowded street and stops in front of us. It's Michael. Emily and Eric exchange a knowing look and head off down the road.

"You better not stop," I say. "The captain might see us talking."

"He's on the ship. I need to talk to you, Nicki."

"Before you say anything," I tell him, "I want you to know, I understand. We don't have to be together. You know, this is just a vacation for me. It's your job, your life."

"But are you OK? I was worried. You didn't look so good yesterday."

"I think I just over-ouzo'd."

"Ios can do that to you—I know from experience."

I sigh. "Listen, Michael. Thank you very much for your kind concern, but I am fine. It's really quite simple. I don't want to mess anything up for you."

He swings his leg over the motorcycle and comes over to me. "I already messed it up. As of yesterday, I'm on probation. And you know what I realized? It's only going to get worse."

"Worse? What do you mean?"

He reaches out, touches the nape of my neck, and leans close. We kiss. And kiss.

"Yeah," I whisper. "I know what you mean. But . . ."

His voice in my ear, soft, with its perfect, clipped syllables: "I have a major policy. I never get involved with passengers. I'm here to concentrate on my work. Period."

"Right. I have no desire to get involved with anybody. I just took this trip because I needed to get away and have a good time."

Michael nods. "OK. So good-bye."

"Good-bye."

Neither of us moves.

"Bye."

"Bye."

"That was just a good-bye kiss," Michael says. "Right?"

"Right." But by now, we are kissing again.

Believe it or not, I've never ridden a motorcycle before. I love the way it feels riding behind Michael, holding on tightly, as if we're escaping from somewhere. We leave the town behind and pass the Black Beach at Kamari, with its dark pebble shore and lineup of blue and white sun umbrellas, then head up the hill, past vineyards, and then we attack a series of hairpin turns. The motorcycle dips precariously from one side to another as we negotiate the twisting road.

"Oh my God, Michael. Maybe we should slow down!"

"We could go up by donkey, you know," he shouts over his shoulder, into the wind.

"The poor donkey!" I close my eyes and bury my head in Michael's shoulder. My hair whips and stings my face. At a grassy area shaded by olive trees, at the top of a rocky cliff, we pull over and stop. Michael props the motorcycle under a huge, gnarled tree that looks like it's hundreds of years old.

"We're here," he announces. Opening a pack on the bike, he pulls out wine and some food wrapped in paper. "Lunch." We lie down under a tree and unwrap the cheese and bread. It's quiet. Very few cars pass by, and the water below the cliff is quiet and clear, like a lagoon.

Looking up through the leafy branches, I realize that I'm feeling something that is very unfamiliar—peace. How long has my life been spent on a hamster wheel, spinning from school to job to whatever, never stopping to think about anything else, mainly because, if I did, I would have to deal with my feelings about my family? It's a new feeling, this restfulness, this being at ease with myself. I like it.

I break off a piece of bread as Michael pours wine into plastic cups. "You know, it seems like I've always been preparing for something, practicing, getting ready. I never had time to do anything real. I was always getting ready for something."

"What?"

"I don't really know. Whatever it was, it never happened."

"Well," says Michael, "You can put things off forever that way, can't you?"

"What do you mean?" I find myself getting defensive. "Waitressing twenty hours a week and taking pre-law isn't exactly putting things off."

He hands me a glass of wine. "But it's not this, is it?"

"Nothing's this." He knew. While he was busy living, I was avoiding life. Or at least life like this. "You seem to know a lot about me, but I don't know anything about you. That's an unfair advantage. I don't even know if you went to college."

He picks up his camera. "This was my university. When I look through it, I'm a student—of nature, people, places. And it's more than that. It's gotten me everything I ever wanted. It got me out of Leeds. It got me here. When you're an artist, you have freedom."

"So I assume you're free from relationships." This is a rhetorical question, but—I realize as soon as I say it—a stupid one. How could a man as attractive as Michael Schuster not be in a relationship? I choke out the words. "Or is there a woman in your life? A girlfriend back home?"

"Worse," he says. "A wife."

A wife. "Oh my God. You're married."

"Wait, wait. *Was* married. That's past tense."

"An ex-wife?"

He nods. "I was twenty-one, she was an eighteen-year-old aspiring model. Unfortunately, her aspirations pretty quickly went beyond me. Well, it wasn't her fault. I found out that neither of us had any business being married. In a way, we used each other. By marrying her, I could pretend I had my own life, that I was independent. And by marrying me, she could pretend she had a career."

I sip my wine. "And now?"

He shrugs. "It's over. Maybe someday I'll be able to focus on what went wrong, but right now I'm trying to concentrate on my work. You can only do so much. But I'll get there. There's no rush, right?"

What can I say? Is this the time to tell him? Forget it. I try to bury the thought, but somehow I am tearing up, and talking is impossible.

"What's wrong?" Michael slips his arm around me.

"Nothing. I just didn't expect this."

"What?"

"To be happy."

"Why not? You're going to law school, you'll be a great lawyer."

"How do you know I'll be anything?"

"I saw it right away, through the camera. You can't fake it for the lens. Nobody can. It sees right through you. You can't hide." He focuses the camera on me. "I see your impatience, your passion, your honesty—not just your beauty."

God. He thinks I'm being honest. Now I really feel like a wretch. "Maybe you don't see everything. What else can you see?"

"I didn't see why you swam out so far and put yourself at risk like that."

"It was an accident."

"You don't seem like the type that has too many accidents. You were very upset by something."

"I got over it. Really. Every once in a while, you know, you have to take some risks. Us being here like this now—that's a risk, isn't it? I think it's time I did some things I hadn't planned."

"You sure?"

"Of course I'm sure."

Michael puts the camera down, jumps up, and grabs my hand. "Then let's go for a swim right now." He pulls me to my feet.

"You've got to be kidding! There's a cliff between us and the ocean."

"Risk, remember." He drags me closer to the edge of the cliff. It's a two-story drop.

"No. I can't."

"Give me one good reason why not?"

"Umm—how about sharks? A major school, circling right at the bottom of this cliff, exactly where I will land. I can't do it."

"Yes you can. I've done it before. I've seen little kids do it from this exact same spot. Just think of it as an extra-high diving board. We'll just jump off and swim back. Look, there are steps, and we can come right back up and do it again. Come on, you can do it." He pulls his T-shirt over his head and kicks off his shoes.

"I'm afraid of heights." I dig in my heels.

"That was yesterday."

"I'll take the stairs down and meet you at the beach."

"Come on, just hold my hand." I step out of my shorts and sandals. "One, two . . . we're going together. You're going with me, right?"

I can do this. Deep breath. "Right."

"Three!" He pulls my hand, and we race to the edge of the cliff and leap off together. Suddenly, I am flying toward the Aegean Sea, screaming and laughing, and I am totally not afraid.

We surface still holding hands, and Michael pulls me closer to him. "See, I told you. You're not afraid of heights."

I shake water from my eyes. "Not anymore."

Have you ever kissed someone in the water? Better still, in the Aegean Sea? It's like kissing in a silk cocoon. For a while we float on our backs, arms out at our sides, fingers barely touching, not talking—just staring up at the sky. Then we swim in to the rocky beach, climb out, and sit in the sun. Michael picks up some stones and skips them across the glassy surface of the water. He hands me one. "It's volcanic," he says. "Perfectly smooth and flat."

"It's a beautiful stone, too pretty to throw back into the water." I clutch the stone and stroke it. Maybe it will bring me luck.

*   *   *

The taste of salt water kisses stay with you a very long time—by comparison, much longer than the taste of kisses on land. That is why, I tell myself, Michael's kisses are still on my lips the day after our daring cliff jump adventure. OK, so I saw a twelve-year-old make the same jump just a few minutes after we did. To me, what I did was a true feat of daring. As were the kisses. Can I tell you what a risk it is to open yourself to love when you know it can never last?

I'm still tasting the kisses as I navigate my way through the labyrinth of the ship to Michael's cabin. I know this is the crew area and I'm not supposed to be here, but most of the crew is on call for the Captain's Dinner, which is tonight. In the cocktail lounge, I noticed Michael wasn't there yet, and I decided to find him. Besides, I want to see his room.

There's a nameplate on his door, so I knock.

"Come in," he yells through the door.

I open it and walk directly into a black sheet. I close the door, pull the sheet aside, and am hit by a wash of red light. Squinting, I see Michael hunched over a small sink in the tiny, crowded space with a single, narrow bunk wedged under an angled wall crowded with photographs. He's developing pictures.

"Hi." I slip my arms around his waist.

"Nick, what are you doing here? It's not a great idea." He turns his head and kisses me anyway, this time on the cheek.

"Is that your work?" Clipped above the sink is a long line of prints. Several of them are shots of me. I see one of me tossing the rose into the ocean, from when the ship left the harbor. How did he take that without me noticing? Or, conversely, just how oblivious had I been?

"Some of these are turning out to be pretty interesting," he says, putting up a large black-and-white of Marie Antoinette.

"This is amazing stuff. Except for those." I point to the shots of me. Now that I look through the red haze, there are pictures of me all over the walls. When did he take all of these?

"Actually, your pictures are my favorites. As for the rest, the jury's out."

I examine the pictures on the walls. Even in the red light, I can see that they are wonderful. But, no matter how good they are, the main thing I can see is how much Michael loves his work. "Michael, you're so talented. Even I can see that, so you must be incredibly talented. And you care so much. What do people say about your work?"

"My commercial stuff—well, they keep hiring

me. As for these, I haven't done much with it yet."

"What are you waiting for?"

"To get my portfolio together, I told you."

"Hm. And how long have you been trying to do that?"

"What's your point, Nicki? This is a process." He impatiently straightens up the sink and flicks the red light off. "I need to be ready. You can't rush it."

"Weren't you the one who was talking to me about getting out there and living your life? There's no point in keeping things to yourself. It doesn't count if nobody sees it."

His jaw tightens.

"You're scared?"

"Why would I be scared? That's ridiculous. Come on. I have to get up to the lounge. The captain will be looking for me."

"Wait a minute." I put my hand on his. "You know, we're all afraid of being rejected. But even if you are, you learn something from it. Look at it this way—it's no worse than jumping off a cliff."

"So I should jump, should I?"

"Jump? You should absolutely leap out there with these pictures. You should throw yourself into the center of the photography world, meet everybody, get an agent, have a show, make your name."

Michael smiles, and then he starts to laugh. "So sayeth my fearless leader."

"Jump, Michael. I promise, you'll survive."

"Well, right now I have to take some party pictures—some couples on the dance floor, a bunch of people smiling over their drinks, a couple of shots of the band, a limbo contest, maybe a still life of the buffet table. Very artistic."

"Stop putting yourself down."

He comes over and takes me in his arms. "You really believe in me, don't you? Maybe it's because you're completely naive about the world of photography. But still, it's nice to listen to the words."

"It's not just words. It's what I believe." I hug him fiercely. "It's the truth. You know it inside, too."

"If I didn't know better, you'd almost make me believe you."

"You'd better believe me. Why wouldn't you?"

"Well, let's just say that to date the reception for my work hasn't been overwhelming. As my ex-wife pointed out when she left after I couldn't get her any magazine covers."

"Magazine covers? So what? Every picture on

these walls—with the exception of a few with a dubious subject—is a hundred times better than any magazine cover I've ever seen. And, excuse me—did she ever think maybe it was her problem?"

He smiled ruefully. "I doubt it."

"Don't do anything for her, or for me, either, for that matter. Don't do this for anybody except one person—yourself." The way I am pushing him surprises me. I know I can't make this man do something about something I know absolutely nothing about—his career. But maybe I'll get him to think about a few things. That would be something, wouldn't it? To make a difference? "Please?"

"Well, since you asked me so nicely . . ."

We kiss, and there it is again—the taste of salt. But this time it's my tears, because I know that whatever happens with Michael, it's never going to be enough to make things whole between us. Quickly, before he can see I'm crying, I bury my head in his shoulder.

Michael flicks the light off in his cabin and we walk into the hall. We know we can't be seen together. He's going to work, I'm going to hang with Eric and Em, and I think we both know we have crossed more than this one doorway.

Chapter 8

One thing about this trip—I'm learning more than I bargained for about these islands. For instance, our two-day stopover at Crete is divided into a day for the beach and a day to tour the ruins of King Minos's palace—home, according to legend, of the infamous half-man-half-bull Minotaur. Emily thinks that this Minotaur creature actually sounds like a lot of guys we know—stubborn, unfeeling, and half-human. "Like Tim, for instance," she says.

I tell her Michael's not like that.

"Right," she says. "He's a god."

The truth is, I'll never know. For me, Michael's a vacation apparition, like the image of a person projected on the screen for the duration of a very entertaining movie, and that's it. This is a relationship that really has nowhere to go, and I know I should just enjoy it for what it is, for the time there is. There can't be more to it. Accept that, girl! Maybe, if I had met him off the ship, off the Aegean, in real life, Michael would turn out to be a Minotaur, too.

Crete is a large island, and there is a secluded beach Michael knows about where nobody from the ship will see us together. By noon, we are lying side by side on striped towels, and Michael's camera, for once, is in its case. Everywhere I look on this beach are families. Parents and kids. Kids and kids. Grandparents. And Michael and me.

"You know," I say, "my parents used to take me to the beach when I was little—before they split up. After that nothing was the same again. Sometimes, I wish I could go back to then. I wish I could time travel and have my family back."

Michael props himself up on his elbow. "But you do have them, don't you?"

"Well, of course I have them. I mean, they're there. I know they love me. But there's just so much baggage. It's hard to deal with it all. All my parents do is argue, and my father basically specializes in making himself scarce."

"How's that?"

"He buries himself in his work."

"You'd never do something like that, right?"

God, he's right. I've been doing the same thing I hate about Dad.

"Maybe you should give them a chance, see what happens."

"Oh, there've been lots of chances. My thirteenth birthday party: Dad didn't make it back from London. Christmas, you name the year—the family tradition was fighting. My high school graduation—Mom had to leave early for a closing."

"Well, you can't be too hard on a single mother. She was basically on her own."

A little boy about Justin's age chases a ball into the surf. "You know, Michael, my stepbrother Justin's about that age, and I've never gone to the beach with him. I barely even know him."

"Well, he's still a baby. You have plenty of time to have a relationship with him."

I can't say anything.

"It's funny," Michael says. "We've both been escaping our families, but for different reasons. Nicki, in the end, all we really have is our families. I see that now. I guess it took leaving Leeds to figure out something that's so basic to life. You should get to know Justin. I had a brother—all we did was fight, but I'd give anything if he were still here." His face is suddenly still.

"What do you mean?"

"I was nine, he was six. Our mother asked me to watch him. We were playing in the front yard and I didn't notice that he wandered off. A car came out of nowhere."

A shiver runs through me, and I touch his arm. "It's not your fault."

"I'll never forgive myself."

"I'm so sorry. Maybe that's the real reason you had to get away."

He sighs. "Maybe. The thing is, you never know what's going to happen. You've got to appreciate people while they're there. Take your little brother to the beach when you get home. And give him a hug for me."

I think about all the hugs I've missed. And, you know, Greece is incredible, Michael is a fabulous guy, but right now, I wish I was at the beach in Evanston, throwing a Frisbee to Justin.

Back on the *Circe*, Emily and Eric are all over me for the details. And I guess I can't blame them—I've been pretty inaccessible. I could tell them how this is the best relationship of my life, how Michael is making me rethink everything I've thought or felt. How he's tapped into something so deep in my soul that I didn't know it even existed. Or how unfair it is that I meet this man when it's too late. But I refuse to do that. If I think about those kinds of things, I'll lose my mind, and, considering the state of affairs, that's one personal accessory I'd better keep my hands on. So, I tell them the only thing I can.

"This is all about having a good time," I tell Emily as I duck into our suite. "That's it. So don't get all fired up."

Emily lights up a cigarette. She's done something really radical with her hair: nothing. It's just combed simply behind her ears. "We just wonder where you are sometimes, that's all."

"Will you put that cigarette out? I can't stand to see you squandering your health. You can't do this anymore."

She stubs out the cigarette. "So now will you tell me what's really going on?"

"Nothing's going on." That much is true, to a point. At night, when I go to sleep, the person in the next bed is Emily.

"Maybe you should take it easy just a bit, Nick. Pace yourself."

"And save myself for what? Let's go. Michael's teaching a windsurfing clinic."

Here's a question: how did I, a totally unathletic person, find myself clinging to a sail, skimming over the waves a mile offshore? Bottom line: if I'm ever going to windsurf, this is it.

Somewhere in the distance, in the direction of shore, is a blur of land. But I'm focusing on simply holding on, my arms clinging to the sail, and leaning my body at the angle that will keep the board from crashing into the waves. I hope Em and Eric are watching at this exact moment, when it looks like I know what I'm doing.

I let go with one hand and wave as I swoop past the swim platform at the stern of the ship, where Emily's hanging over the rail and Michael's in a skiff by the swim platform, taking pictures.

The next thing I know, the board whips out from under my feet, the sail wrenches from my hands, and I crash into the water, grazing my head on the board. For a long second, I'm dazed, lost underwater, disoriented, and then I feel a yank at the back of my T-shirt as Michael pulls me up into the skiff like a mother cat pulling on the nape of her kitten's neck. Sputtering, I surface. "What happened?"

"The wind shifted."

"Nicki! Are you all right?" It's Eric, swimming to us from his own board. "God, she's bleeding!"

"She hit her head on the board," Michael says.

My windsurfer is lying sideways in the water, the sail like a burst balloon.

I reach up to my stinging forehead. My hand comes away bloody.

"Let's get her back to the ship," snaps Eric, climbing into the skiff.

"It's just a little bump on the head," I protest.

"Let me see." Eric pushes back my hair and peers at my head. "Seems like a surface cut. They can be bleeders. Your pupils aren't dilated. But why don't you get out, take it easy the rest of the day, maybe check with the ship's doctor."

My forehead stings, but otherwise I feel fine. "Why would I want to do that?"

"I really think she's fine," says Michael.

"Oh, and you're an expert. Listen, Michael, you're pushing her too hard."

"It's just a little accident. It happens all the time. I really don't see your problem."

"I'm getting back up," I say, trying to right the board. "This has to be like riding a bike, you have to get right back up if you fall off. Now if you gentlemen will excuse me . . ."

"Nick . . ." Eric pleads, reaching out for me.

"Let her go," Michael cuts him off. "She's not hurt, she wants to do it, she's a grown-up. What's with you?"

I leave them both in the water as I struggle to my feet on the board.

"Watch your feet," Michael says. "Point the board into the wind while you bring up the sail."

I follow his directions, the sail catches the wind, and I'm off. In a minute, I may fall again, but, for the moment, I own the sea and the sky.

After the windsurfing session, I take a shower, put a Band-Aid on my cut, squeeze in a nap, and set off to catch up with Michael. I have to search practically the whole boat before I find him in the gym, taking shots of a yoga class.

"I can't believe I slept through lunch," I say. "But it's not too late to catch the shuttle in to the ruins. You're going, right?"

The camera whirrs. "I don't think so. I have some layouts to finish. I've gotten way behind." That's when I hear the irritation in his voice.

"Wait a minute. You make it sound like it's my fault."

Michael pushes his hair off his face and stands staring at me. His eyes look guarded and distant. Why? "It's not a matter of fault. I just have things to finish up." He reaches into his vest and pulls out some more film.

Unbelievable. If I didn't know better, I'd think there was a problem.

"You're not telling me everything. I thought

we were going to be honest with each other."

"We can't have this discussion here." Michael takes my arm and walks me out of the gym. Then he turns to face me and looks straight into my eyes. "I thought we were going to be honest with each other, too, Nicole, but clearly that hasn't been the case."

He looks so terribly hurt. I feel my stomach clench. "What are you saying?"

"Emily told me everything."

Thank you, Emily, for ruining my life, or what I have left of it. At this moment, I feel a thousand times worse than I did in the hospital. My God, he knows. I can see it on his face. And what must he think of me? Sick, dying, and worse—a liar, if not outright, by omission. "And, it makes a difference?" I whisper.

"Of course it does. Did you honestly think it wouldn't? My God, Nicki, why didn't you tell me?"

"I guess I thought we'd just go along like we were."

"Well, under the circumstances, it's not going to go very far, is it?"

I have a whole speech prepared in my head, the same speech I've had waiting since the beginning of this relationship, even since before. Actually, it's a script that I made up in the hospital for just such occasions as this, when I'd be exposed for what I am—an impostor impersonating a healthy person, a human dead end masquerading as someone with a future. But when you're in the hospital, you don't realize that scripts like that don't work on the outside. Nothing does. But if Michael can't handle it, I don't want any more to do with him than he wants to do with me.

"OK, fine," I say. "And thank you, Michael Schuster, for showing me the kind of person you really are." I mean it, too. And I leave.

First stop after I storm out of Michael's cabin— Emily. I find her out on the deck in a lounge chair, playing backgammon with Shirley.

"Emily, I have to talk to you."

She doesn't look up. "Not now. I'm doubling."

"Double-crossing is more like it." I can't help myself. I look at this woman, supposedly my best friend. A traitor with an ankle tattoo.

Emily looks up at me from the corner of her eye, but she says nothing.

"Answer me. I know you talked to him."

Emily squirms. She's always been a disaster under pressure.

"I can't believe you told him. You promised."

Shirley shakes the cup and rolls the dice. "Doubles!" she announces.

"Time out," Emily says to Shirley. Then she stands up and faces me. "I didn't say anything."

"Don't lie to me."

Shirley shakes her head. "Girls, girls, men are never worth fighting over. Have a margarita instead. It's much healthier."

Yeah, I'm on a health kick. The idea makes me laugh, and I can't help myself—I start laughing hysterically, tears spilling onto my cheeks. Eric, who hates the sun and has been inside watching satellite TV, notices us through the window. So now he'll come over, too. Great: recipe for a scene. Concern in his voice, Eric touches my shoulder. "Nick, is everything all right?"

"She told him, Eric."

"What?"

"Everything. I can't believe she'd do this to her best friend, can you?"

Emily runs her fingers through her hair: a sure sign of guilt. She always does this when she's on the spot. "Nicki, listen. It's not what you think."

"What else is there to think? He knows I'm dying. He can't deal. Just like Tim." What other outcome could I expect?

Emily starts to cry. "I swear to you, I didn't tell him that. I only mentioned Tim because I was trying to help you."

135

I am totally confused. "Tim? Help?"

Em nods sorrowfully. "I didn't mean for anything bad to happen."

"Wait a minute. Tim?"

Eric holds up his hand. "Nicki, Emily didn't tell Michael about your health. She was just trying to get you to relax—misguidedly, maybe, but you've got the wrong impression here."

"I only thought you needed a little downtime, Nick," Emily pleads. "You haven't stopped for one second since you met Michael. I knew you weren't going to cut back—I know you—so I thought maybe it could be Michael that arranged for a little breathing room."

"Right. And where does Tim fit into all this?"

"I—I didn't know what to tell Michael. I ended up making up something about Tim and you somehow. I didn't plan it, it just sort of blurted out. It wasn't really about Tim, either, it was about coming up with a reason for Michael to give you some space, so you could relax and get better." She sniffles into her wrist. "I guess it backfired." She grabs my hand. "Can you ever forgive me, Nick?"

We're both crying now, and I think Eric is on the verge. I can't believe this. We go on this trip together, best friends, just so we can have the best time ever, and be together, and now we're in tears and making each other feel miserable. Instead of growing closer, we're losing touch with each other. Or, more precisely, I've lost touch with my friends. Can I tell you something? I think that's one of the bigger downsides of being fatally ill. You become terminally self-centered, because you know that in the foreseeable future, there will be no you. OK, Nicki, I tell myself, you've used your best friends like a couple of human hat racks—you drop in, toss them a comment, and take off.

Am I wrong, or does it all sound familiar? Maybe I'm good at it because I've practiced. On my family.

"Em, Eric—I'm so sorry. I guess I didn't think about how hard it is for you guys, too. When I dragged you out here, I was only thinking about myself. I didn't stop to think about anybody else. This can't be easy for you, either. I think it's you guys who are going to have to forgive me."

We all put our arms around each other. "No big deal, Nick," says Emily, with a hug.

But I know it is.

"So, are you going to tell Michael?" asks Eric.

"I—don't know. God, this is so hard. Sometimes I think living is harder than dying, you know?" OK, I did it—used the D Word. But once I say it out loud, it's not so frightening.

Shirley taps Eric on the shoulder with a lacquered fingernail. "Did I miss something here? Who's dying?"

I look her directly in the eye.

She gets it.

I'm not the nap type, but I'm exhausted after all this. I collapse onto the bed and Eric gives me some meds. They knock me out, and when I wake up, it's the next day and we're in Symi, a small, craggy island, and our next stop on the cruise. Out the cabin window, I see the rectangular-shaped, whitewashed harbor town and a multicolored clutter of pleasure and fishing boats. But there's really only one person I want to see.

Michael is on deck, working with the water taxi crew.

"Michael . . ." I want to see him alone, but he's obviously working. He's got his camera and the big bag, and he's helping passengers onto the shuttle.

"Michael, we need to talk."

"Look," he says brusquely, "it doesn't matter." His eyes brush mine and then look away. He hands an armful of canvas bags and backpacks down into the shuttle. Very professional.

"Still, we need to talk."

"Yeah, we do. I've been doing some thinking. The shuttle is leaving for Agios Nikolaos. We can talk there. I'm off at dinnertime." He gives me the name of a harbor-front restaurant. I'm to meet him there. The shuttle takes off, and as I stand there watching it head toward shore, Michael turns around and looks at me. That's when I know that there's still something there, something that can't be severed. We'll work it out. I know it.

I was going to tell him. I really was. True, when you are sitting with the man you love in an intimate, candlelit taverna, the *Circe* at anchor in the distance, glittering from stern to mast with thousands of lights, the atmosphere is set for romance, not confession, but we will just ignore all that for now.

The waiter pours our wine. "You have to try the dried octopus," says Michael.

I'd eat Moby Dick if Michael recommended it.

The waiter leaves and we are alone. I take a deep breath.

"I really wanted to talk to you, Nicki," Michael says, taking my hand. "I felt really bad about everything. But you should know something."

"Actually, Michael, can I say something?"

"I don't want to hear any apologies from you. None. Because you are right."

"What?"

"I've been on a bit of an edge over something you said to me. You struck a nerve, like nobody has, ever."

I rack my brain—what did I say?

"You're right, Nicki. I can do it. And I have a new plan—thanks to you. I'm going to have studios in New York and in London. An international client base. After all, I already have a foot in both worlds. Of course, I'll be travelling constantly for the next few years, setting the groundwork, but in the end, it'll be worth it, don't you think?"

What am I going to say—go ahead, Michael, set up your business, become a big success, but don't mind me, I'll be the one that's not there to see it? Instead I say, "Definitely worth it." And I smile.

"If everything works out, you could practice at one of the big firms in New York, couldn't you?"

"Theoretically." I sip my wine. Well, I'm not lying. I would never lie to Michael. Tell the truth, but not the whole truth.

"So, Nick, maybe we're on the same timetable?"

"I don't really live by timetables anymore."

"Exactly! There's always tomorrow, right?"

"Right. I just like to enjoy what I'm doing when I'm doing it. Like being with you now. That's enough for me."

He squeezes my hand, but I'm feeling a bit numb.

"But it's fun to fantasize about the future. What do you see yourself doing in five years? Do you want to have kids, or is it all career?"

Kids. The thought knocks the wind out of me. I see a little girl with Michael's hair and eyes. A boy with my mother's nose. Ruby and Alex. I can't sustain the image; they're gone. "I can't think about children," I whisper.

He nods. "I know what you mean. Once, I thought I'd have a family by now. Now, it seems a long way off."

The waiter puts down our plates, but food isn't on Michael's mind yet.

"For a long time, I thought I'd be a mother," I say. "Can you believe it? I even named my kids—Ruby and Alex."

"Sure, you'd make a great mom." He grins.

I shake my head. "Now, no. My plans have changed. It's not important."

"Career girl to the end."

"You—might say that." I reach for my wine,

but it's dark, things are fuzzy. My glass clatters over and shatters. Michael jumps up and pulls back my chair.

"Are you all right?"

I stand up and brush off the broken glass. "Fine, just a little tired."

"Somebody's been keeping you out too late."

The waiter appears and whisks off the table-cloth.

"You know, Nick, I've been thinking," Michael says as we settle back down at the freshly dressed table. "When the cruise is over, why don't you swing back through London with me. Meet my family?"

Now what? Tell him. But I say, "I'd love to, but I really need to get home."

Michael traces my cheek with his thumb. "Maybe I can change your mind." He lifts his glass and hands me mine. "To tomorrow."

What can I say? Our glasses touch softly. "Tomorrow."

Chapter 9

"*It's* a surprise," says Michael.

The four of us are hurtling along in one of the *Circe*'s Jeeps on Symi, where on this day some mysterious festival is taking place. Michael's going to photograph it, and we've been invited along. We pass beautiful, red-trimmed neoclassical houses with red tile roofs that look down on the postcard views of the harbor. The day's washing flaps from lines that crisscross between buildings, and magnificent white stairways climb the hillside, linking the houses with the harbor. Tall cypress trees stick straight upward as if they were dropped like darts into the ground.

"Ha! Mystery solved!" crows Emily triumphantly. She waves a guidebook, then holds it ostentatiously open. "And I quote: 'Every year,

143

each of the island's single girls puts a ring on a large plate, from which an elderly woman picks the name of her future husband." She smiles— her calculated look. "I want to get in line. Who has a ring?"

"Do you think it's too late to call Shirley? She'd pay big money for this kind of information."

"Does Shirley qualify as a single girl?" asks Emily.

"Which? The single or the girl?" Eric commandeers the guidebook. "You'll like this part. After the ceremony, the women eat cake and pour wine into themselves until they're wasted."

"My kind of ceremony." Em taps me on the shoulder. "Here I'm in residence on the Love Boat and so far nobody has even made a pass at me. This calls for drastic measures, and if I have to eat cake and get wasted, so be it. So who goes first, you or me?"

As we approach the church of Agios Athanassious, I can see a quarter-mile-long line of girls and young women in every sort of dress, heads covered, lined up at the church steps. "Count me out," I say. "I think I'll stay in the car."

"Sure, Nick, I'll stay with you," says Em quickly.

"And miss out on the name of your future husband? No way. You owe it to your public. Go."

Michael stops the car, but Em doesn't move. "I'm staying with Nicki," she says.

"Come on," Michael says, standing up in the Jeep and snapping a series of shots. "Don't you want to know the name of your future husband?"

"I'm not into the future," I say.

"Maybe it works on men," Eric says, jumping out of the car. "Come on, Em, let's break some centuries-old traditions. See what the old bag says when I ask her what my future husband's name will be."

Emily arches an eyebrow. "I hate to disappoint you, Eric, but I think that's a tradition that started around here."

"Why don't you guys go ahead," Michael says. "I'll take Nicki to the next town, and we'll come back and meet you after lunch."

"Michael, what about your pictures?" I ask. "You go with them."

"The place I have in mind is even better," he says.

He's right. We drive up the hill about five miles to the ruins of an ancient village, and that's where we stop. All I can do is stare.

"This is amazing, Michael. Just think, this place has been here thousands of years before us, and it'll still be here thousands of years after we're gone."

"And all of them left their footprints, some-how. You can feel it, can't you?"

Leaving footprints. That's what I want to do.

We pull over at a lookout point and walk up two long flights of stairs into a huge courtyard. The space is ringed with crumbling columns.

"This was a temple to Aphrodite," Michael says.

"The goddess of love."

We're alone, and Michael puts his arm around me and we stand quietly.

"Michael, I really have to tell you something right now."

"No, Nicki, I have to tell you. I've been think-ing about it a lot. Ever since we jumped off that cliff, I've felt like I'm still falling, and where I'm falling is into your arms."

I bury my head in the crook of his neck. "Mi-chael, I just can't."

"Why not?" He strokes my hair. "Is it that other guy after all? You're still thinking about him?"

"Oh, God, no," I gasp. "I haven't even thought about him once."

"Well, I won't pressure you. We've got all the time in the world." He kisses my forehead. "But I need to know one thing. How do you feel about me? Do you think you could spend the rest of your life with me?"

That and more, Michael. "No problem." We kiss before I can say any more.

We are in bed when it happens. Michael and I are in my room, naked, lying in pools of moonlight. My dress that I was going to wear to dinner is on the floor. Michael is so full of passion, it's like making love with him will infuse me with a measure of his life. I am selfish, I know. I take and take. He doesn't seem to mind.

He's lying with his arm across me, asleep, when my head is pierced by a glass shard—or at least that's how it feels. I'm jolted awake with a blinding, familiar pain.

Not yet. Please.

Have you ever tried to bargain with pain? Let me tell you, pain is a tough customer. I offer frantic deals: total elimination of all vices, dedication of myself to the less fortunate, anything. Pain will have none of it. Its goal: my head on a plate.

I have to get out of here. Pulling back the

covers carefully, I climb out on my side. Michael doesn't move, which is what I want. He can't see me. He can't see this. He won't.

The bathroom. That's my goal. If I can make it to the bathroom, I can get to my medicine. And a door to shut.

I don't make it. The moon suddenly blinks and goes dark, like a burned-out bulb.

It's not the moon, it's me: I am blind. I can only stand here in pitch darkness with my head on fire. I squeeze my skull, hoping to eliminate the pain, brutalize it. But I can't even tell which of my medicines are which.

I feel my way along the wall to the bathroom door, put on the long robe I know is hanging on the hook there, and go hand over hand back along the wall to the door to the hall. The minute I'm out there, I stumble and fall, skinning my knees. But I know Eric and Em are in Eric's room, so I crawl next door.

"Miss, may I help you?"

I can't see who is talking to me. But he solves that problem by introducing himself. "I'm First Officer Pevin." He puts his hands under my arms and lifts me to my feet.

"I'm fine." I pound on Eric's door.

I hear Emily inside. "Who is . . ." She yanks the door open. "Oh my God!" she shrieks when she sees me.

Then I hear Michael's voice as he opens the door of my suite down the hall. "Nicki?"

I literally fall into Eric's room, and Emily slams the door behind me. I know there is a commotion in the hall behind me, but now all I can think of is this pain. "Eric, Em, it's back!" I start to sob. "Don't tell Michael."

"Nicki!" I hear Michael yelling in the hall.

"What is it, Nick? Do you need a doctor?" Eric holds on to my arm as if his grip were a life ring.

"I can't see," I whisper, curling into a ball.

He picks me up, carries me, and gently puts me down on his bed. "Emily, get my bag. I've got a set of Nicki's medications in there."

I hear clattering and crashing from the bathroom, and I don't have to see to know that Emily is knocking things into the sink and onto the floor as she searches for some magic pills. I hear her wail, "Oh shit oh shit oh shit!" Finally, water runs, and I hear her footsteps as she bounds back into the bedroom.

"Nicki," says Eric, as calmly as if he were telling me what channel he was choosing on the TV, "let me help you sit up. I have three pills here." He presses them into my hand, one at a time, and a glass appears at my lips. My hand is shaking and the water slops onto my face and dribbles down my neck, but I manage to take the pills. How long till they take effect? I know they won't stop the blindness—there's no pill for that—but, please, the headache.

"This should help with the pain. The cortisone will reduce the internal swelling you must be having. But you need to see your doctors." His tone is sober. We all know what this means. I accept it. What I don't accept is the timing.

"Eric, we've got to get her to the hospital," Emily whispers, as if I'm not in the room.

"There's one in Athens. I'll call the ship's doctor."

"No, wait!" I can't go to Athens. "I want to go home."

A knock on the door—a pounding, actually.

"Nicki, are you in there?"

Michael.

Emily's hand is on mine. "Should I let him in?" she asks.

I want to shake my head no, but it hurts to move. "No, don't let him in. He can't see me like this."

"Are you sure?" she says. "He cares about you. Maybe you want him here."

"No!"

Emily squeezes my hand. "She's not in here."

Through the door, I hear Michael's voice. "I can't find Nicole. Can I come in?"

"I'm not dressed," Emily calls back. "I'm—entertaining."

We all hold our breath collectively until he's gone.

"Nicki, when are you gonna tell this guy?" Eric asks.

"Never." I know it wouldn't matter anyway. Yes, I am being selfish, or worse, but at this moment the love of that man is the only thing I've got left, and this is how I want to remember it.

Somehow, I make it through the longest night I will ever know, a night without sight, sleep, or sense. Eric and Emily talk to me, tell funny stories, hold me, and basically keep me alive, even though there are many moments when I would much rather die than face what certainly lies ahead. The worst is morning, which finally, finally comes, and with it, the fact that I am leaving the ship and the man I never want to live without. Forever.

The sun, supposedly, is out, but to me it's still a thousand shades of black when we leave the ship. Did anybody ever tell you that blindness is not as simple as plain pitch black? It's every shade of black you've ever known, or been terrified to imagine—the dangerous black of being locked in a car trunk; the onerous black of a power failure; the senseless black of passing out; the bone-chilling black of your worst nightmare. They've all joined forces, and they're here together, inside my skull. Luckily, my headache has abated enough that I can walk, if somebody holds my arm and we advance very slowly. I will block out of my mind the fact that I had to be dressed by Emily, like a helpless baby. I don't even know if she packed my clothes or hers. Eric makes the arrangements, and, after a pointless examination by the ship's doctor, I stick a pair of sunglasses on my face, hide my nonseeing eyes behind them, and we leave the ship.

Every step as we head for the water taxi, I expect to hear Michael, or feel his touch. But nothing. I don't want him to come, but at the same time, I do. The thought that I will never be with Michael again is much harder to deal with than being sick again. Without Michael, I feel frightened and vulnerable again. But at the same time, I know it would be totally selfish to involve him in my life. And I have to face it now: this is my life, or what is left of it.

Just as well that Michael doesn't come.

"What are you telling people?" I ask Eric as he helps me, one step at a time, board the shuttle.

"That we've decided to leave the ship and go

home. This isn't school, Nick, you don't have to have an explanation for leaving."

The boat rocks, and I struggle to keep my equilibrium. Who wouldn't?

Every time I've taken this water taxi from the *Circe* to the shore, something wonderful awaited me. This final time, I dread the trip. The boat ride is silent except for the drone of the motor. At the Symi dock, I don't need to see the activity around us to hear and sense it. There is a sudden loss of peace and leisure, and, in its place, the commercial clamor, cacophony of voices, and imposed sense of purpose. At the harbor, we transfer to a commercial ferry, which takes us to Crete, where we will take a small plane to Athens, and finally, from there, a flight home.

Emily strokes my hand as the ferry plows along. "It's going to be OK, Nick. They'll fix you up once you get home."

"Did you see Michael anywhere?"

"No, honey, we didn't."

I lean my head on Em's shoulder. I feel more tired than I've ever been in my life, and I drop off to sleep to the drone of the ferry engine.

We eventually get to Crete, and Eric and Em help me off the ferry.

"You two wait here by the dock with the luggage," says Eric. "I'm going to get a taxi."

He returns with the taxi and escorts me into the backseat while he and Em load the bags.

I'm sitting there when I hear my name— "Nicki! Nicki!"

Michael.

"He's here," Eric says. "Nick, you won't believe this, he's in the back of a truck with a bunch of goats. He looks like shit. Probably smells like it, too, from the looks of things. God, where's he been?"

"OK," says Emily, "figure out what you want to do, Nick. He's coming closer, he's waving frantically. He definitely sees us."

"We have a plane to catch," I say firmly, mustering all my resolve.

"Nicki, where were you?" Michael's hand is on my shoulder. Oh my God. "Why are you going home? They told me on the boat—well, anyhow, something has happened and I have to talk to you."

I hide behind my sunglasses.

"Hiya, Mike. Taken up goatherding in your spare time?" Eric jibes.

"Nobody's talking to you," Michael says. "Nicki, what in God's name is wrong? Did I do something? Tell me."

"Nothing's wrong."

"Then why won't you look at me?"

"I can't." Truth. "Look, I just need some time to sort things out, OK?"

"Nicki, the captain fired me. That asshole George, he saw me leaving your cabin. That did it. They threw me off the boat last night. Then, this morning, I called the boat to find you and they told me you were headed for Crete. I had to hitch a ride on a fishing boat to get here, but they had engine trouble and they came in to the next port down. A big cruise ship had just come in and I couldn't get a taxi, so I talked my way into the back of the truck with the goats. So, if you're really leaving, we can be together. I'll come with you. Or you'll come with me."

That stops me. "Michael, that's awful about your job, and I'm so sorry, but it's complicated. We can't be together any more, just believe me. I have to go home."

"I thought we needed each other. I thought we were together."

Breathe, girl. Keep it together. "I have to go now. I can't talk to you."

He grabs my arm away from Emily. "I don't get it. Why are you being like this?"

"Calm down, man. Didn't you hear the lady? She needs breathing room." Eric peels Michael's hand off my arm.

"This is none of your business," Michael says fiercely. "Nicki?"

"It's over, Michael."

"That's a lie, and you know it."

I can feel his breath, hot on my face. He is looking at me, blocked by my sunglasses.

"It's not a lie," I whisper. "Ask me if I love you, and I'll tell you yes."

I wish I could throw myself into your arms. It's unimaginable that I can't see your face now, one last time. Touch you, kiss you, feel you against me, where you belong. I have to accept that can never happen. But I won't forget a single centimeter of your face or your body. Not as long as I live, whether that's five more minutes or a hundred and fifty years.

Even through my pain, horror, and fear, I know this much: This is how it feels to walk away from the man you never want to leave. I slam the taxi door and tell the driver to step on it.

It's bizarre how it feels to be guided through the airport like a handicapped person. Wait, did I say like a handicapped person?

Eric is the optimistic one. "Listen, Nick, don't forget—this isn't going to be permanent. Your doctor said the steroids would kick in and reduce the swelling that's on the optic nerve, and then you'd get your sight back. Once you're home and they can ramp up with the IV, you'll turn this thing around."

Emily says, "I can see the plane outside the window—a prop job."

Our flight is announced over the speaker.

"That's us," says Emily as she touches my elbow, and we stand up together. "We'll be going outside," she says, "and then there's a stairway."

"Miss McBain?" says a woman's voice, in English with a Greek accent.

"Yes."

"I'm from special services. Allow me to help you pre-board the flight."

We walk slowly out onto the tarmac. A light rain has begun to fall. The agent's high heels tap a pattern on the pavement, and garbled sounds squawk from her walkie-talkie, or maybe they just sound garbled because I don't understand Greek.

"You know," says Eric, the resident master of diversion, "the first thing I want to do when I get home is order a hamburger with all the sides."

"The first thing I want to do is get a hot stone massage," says Emily. "And get a dog. I'm through with men. They don't appreciate me. I'm moving on to animals."

157

The first thing I want to do is kiss Justin. I can't believe how much I suddenly miss that kid. He doesn't know it, but he's about to become the man in my life.

As we start up the airplane stairs, slowly, one step at a time, I hear the footsteps of people running toward the plane—footsteps, then a voice. "Nicki!"

Michael.

"Sir!" a man's voice shouts after him. "Passengers only at this point. Do you have a ticket?"

"Oh my God," says Emily.

"Nicki?" Eric asks, waiting for my direction, but I have no idea what to do or say. The metal staircase shudders as he pounds up the steps. I am still wondering what to say when his arms are around me. "Nicki, just tell me what I did. What's wrong? I know something isn't right. What did I do?"

You fell in love with a woman with an inoperable brain tumor who is going home to die, that's what you did, Mr. Michael Schuster. And she fell in love with you. And now, after you have given her so much, she is going to give you the best gift she has to give: your escape. "You made me love you. That's what you did. And I can't. That's what's wrong and that's the end of it. Now please leave me alone. You have to leave me alone." I can feel the tears beneath my sunglasses.

"No, Nicole. You made me love you. So can't we work this out?"

"I'm sorry." This, I know, is worse than dying. Or maybe it is dying. I am killing us both.

"What the hell is 'sorry'?"

Eric intercedes. "The lady told you once, she told you again."

"Shut up," Michael barks.

"Sir," says the agent, "you must get off the stairway. Passengers need to board, and it's against regulations . . ."

"Get your hands off me!"

"Sir, you are creating a disturbance and a safety hazard. I must call security."

Michael's arms go limp and fall away from me. "There's no need for that," he says, his voice horribly quiet. "Good-bye, Nicole."

As I walk up the remaining steps to the plane, I hear Michael's steps retreat. Then I am on the plane, belted in a seat within a metal fortress. I lean my head against the window porthole and sob into my blackness.

Chapter 10

*O*ne week later, the Aegean has been re-placed by Lake Michigan, the beaches of Santorini by Lincoln Park, and, amazingly, I can see again. The doctors have worked their steroid magic once again. But they have also warned me that this is only temporary. Of course, they tried again to lock me up, and again I refused. In the spirit of compromise, I agreed to rest when I'm dead. Right now, I have way too much to do.

Dad and I took Justin to the zoo and the duck pond, and now we're on the swings at the play-ground. Justin and I share one swing—he's on my lap—and Dad is next to us. It is a contest. Who can touch the sky first?

"No fair," laughs Dad, pumping away, "it's two against one."

"No excuses, right, Justin?" I yell. We swing

higher and higher, and he giggles wildly. This is great. How much have I missed by not doing it before? How dumb and selfish was I? At least, I have Michael to thank for this.

We win the contest, and Justin leaps from my lap and dashes off across the playground.

"Don't go too far!" I call after him.

"Just to the sandbox!" he chirps back.

Dad smiles. He hasn't smiled much lately. It looks good on him. "Justin loves being with you, Nicki. He's always worshiped you, you know. I know he can be rough, if you're not used to kids, but he's young, and . . ."

"Dad, forget it. I was the one being a baby, not him."

"Well, I'm glad you guys are getting to know each other."

"I was stupid not to spend more time with him before. He's such a great kid."

"Well, you can spend all the time you want with him now," Dad says, keeping one eye on Justin as he busies himself by the sandbox.

"I just don't want to make him sad. He can't handle what's happening with me."

"I wouldn't worry. Kids handle things better than we do sometimes." He gets off and walks behind my swing and pushes it. "You know, I used to do this when you were a little girl."

I smile, remembering. Just a few weeks ago, I would have had a comeback crack, but now I'm content to know that we had that time, once, and it was great.

"So tell me about this guy Michael," Dad says. "You left messages about him for both your mother and me on our voice mails. What's the deal with him?"

"Dad, if only I'd met him another time, any other time. Or if things had been different. He was the greatest guy. We had more together on that trip than I've ever really had in my life."

"I see," says Dad.

"He's the first guy that really got to me, ever. You know, we could have spent the rest of our lives together—if this was another life."

Dad rubs my shoulder. "I'm sorry, honey. That's rough. It must have been hard for him, too."

"In a different way. He thinks I dropped him. He didn't know anything. I didn't tell him. The thing is, he loved me for who I am."

Justin scampers back, like a puppy on the loose. "Nicki! Nicki! Come here! I have something to show you!"

A little hand reaches up and tugs. I get off the swing, and we dash together across the playground to a bench by the sandbox. Justin's backpack is there, surrounded by paper and crayons. "Look," he says. "I made some drawings." He holds up one of a stick figure.

"What's that?"

"You on the swing. I made it for you."

I pick it up and admire it. "It's beautiful, Justin. Thank you." I lean over to kiss him and notice another drawing on the bench. A black heart. "This one is very pretty, too, Jussie. But why is the heart black?"

He stares at the ground.

"Justin?"

His voice is tiny. "Because I'm sad."

So.

"You know, Justin," I try to say this carefully. "If someone loves you, they never really leave you, no matter what."

He looks at me suspiciously. "Really?"

"It's true," I say firmly, and, leaning over, I whisper in his ear. "There's a magic secret."

Now I've got his attention. "Magic? Secret?"

"If you just think of the person, they will always be there in your heart, giving you a secret hug that will make you happy. That's the thing about love. The other person doesn't have to be there for you to feel it. I'll show you—close our eyes, and this is what you'll feel."

Justin squeezes his eyes tight shut, and I give

him a great big bear hug. I don't want to let go, but I do.

"Now open your eyes."

He does.

"OK, that's how it will always feel. Got it?"

Justin nods.

"I love you, Jussie." I give him another hug.

"Me too," says a small voice.

"Now," I put him at arm's length. "I think I see the ice cream truck over there. Here's some money." I hand him a five dollar bill. "Why don't you go get some popsicles for us."

"Can I have a Calippo?"

"Whatever you want."

Off he races. As I watch him run, I wonder, does he understand any of what I told him? I think it doesn't matter in fact if he understood my words, as long as he got the feeling behind them. But, with kids, how can you know?

"What did you guys talk about?" asks Dad.

"Art. I wish I'd played with Justin more, Dad. I'm sorry."

"Justin loves you, honey. He's your brother. No matter how much or how little you play with him, that's not going to change."

"Kind of like fathers and daughters, huh?"

"You might say that."

We swing for a while, and for a change, it's a comfortable silence.

"Nicki! Nicki!" Justin tumbles across the grass, waving a Calippo in one hand and a piece of paper in the other and throwing himself into my arms. "It worked!"

"What worked, Jussie?"

He proudly hands me the piece of paper. On it is a drawing of a heart, colored red, yellow, pink, and orange.

"See?" I say, and we smile at each other, sharing our special secret.

Dad examines the paper and shrugs. "Nice drawing. But did I miss something here?"

No, Dad. I was the one who missed something.

The next day, Emily and I decide to go for a walk by the harbor, but she shows up with company—her new basset hound puppy, Samson. With the dog on a leash and her cashmere twinset, Emily looks like she's channeling Grace Kelly.

"So, Em, what happened to the boutique you were going to open?" The wind is chilly today, whipping the lake into gray whitecaps, a harbinger of fall.

"New plan," she announces, dodging a biker. "I'm going to work with animals instead. Much more loving than sportswear. Right, Samson?"

It's amazing how Emily ascribes human intelligence to this dog. She gives him more credit than most of her boyfriends.

"Emily," I say, "I want you to know that the one thing that means everything to me right now is having my friends. I could never handle this alone."

"You're beyond human, Nick. You're handling this great. I don't know how you do it."

Neither do I, Emily. But I say, "In a funny way, I've learned to live with what I have, or don't have. It's strange, but when it seems like you have forever, nothing's important. And now I see that what's important was always here, around me. Except for maybe one thing."

"What's that? We'll work on it."

"It's a person."

"Oh. So why don't you call him?"

I duck my head into the wind. It feels like my face is being sandblasted. Chicago has to have the worst reputation on the planet for wind—deservedly. "I must think of calling Michael twenty times a day, but I always stop myself," I admit to Emily. "If I called him, I'd have to admit that I lied to him. He may remember me as a bitch, but that's a step up from a liar."

"Nicki, are you sure?" Emily says. "He really seemed to care about you."

"Well, I'd much rather have him think of me as a normal person with some problems than a charity case he has to pity. God, think of Tim. Pity is not love. At least I know Michael loved me. That's something."

"Speaking of Tim..." says Emily. "Twelve o'clock due north."

A rollerblader is heading toward us on the path.

Tim.

He sees us before we see him, and he slows down when he reaches us, turns and skates up next to me. Samson skitters excitedly.

"Hey, Nick, I heard you were back."

"Hi Tim," I manage.

"Tim, what a coincidence," Emily says, her voice dripping with sarcasm.

He smiles a bit foolishly. Emily's new, clean-cut style inspires a double take. "Emily, you look so... different. So... normal. Actually, I called Lori. She said you guys were at the park. It's great seeing you, Nick."

I'm hardly won over. "I'm still alive, if that's what you mean."

"You missed a great cruise, Tim," Emily says, yawning. "You should have come. Then again, maybe it's good that you didn't—right, Nick?"

I sidestep. "Well, we had fun."

"You look terrific," Tim says.

"How deep," Emily yawns.

I wonder if this is going to get ugly. I know that Eric and Emily never got over Tim's defection, but I've had to move on. "It's OK, Em," I whisper, putting my hand on her arm. "Can I talk to Tim alone? Would you mind?"

She gives Tim a withering look. "Samson, I can tell when we're not wanted. Heel!" She peels off with the dog.

Tim skates slowly alongside me, his eyes on the ground. "So Greece was great, huh?"

"Yeah, pretty great."

There's an awkward silence. Then Tim clears his throat. "Nick, you have to know—I feel really bad about what happened. I want you to know."

I sigh. "Tim, the one thing I don't want to do is talk about the past. How's work?"

"Crazy, but I like it. They actually incorporated a couple of my ideas in the plans. Nick, do you think we could have lunch? I don't want to leave things the way they are."

"Which is?"

"I just feel like such a shit."

"Maybe that's because you were such a shit."

"I just couldn't deal. But I've worked it out. You'll see."

Sure I see, it's all about you, Tim. But so what. I'll humor him. "I'm glad you feel better, Tim. Now for lunch."

"Where do you want to go?"

I see a hot dog vendor. "There."

We get dogs with all the trimmings from the cart, and chips, and settle on a park bench.

"I heard you met somebody on the trip," says Tim casually, opening his chips. Yes, he's been talking to my mother.

"It wasn't just somebody."

"Serious, huh?" Tim jokes, expecting me to say no. Maybe expecting something else, too.

"You know, when I was a little girl, I always dreamed of being a bride. I knew exactly what my gown would be like—off the shoulder, sparkly little pearls, a train." I'm talking more to myself than to Tim now. "I'd wear a veil, I'd carry lilies of the valley. The bridesmaids would wear pink, with flowers in their hair. There'd be a flower girl, throwing rose petals from a little white wicker basket. For dinner, we'd have lobster. A chocolate wedding cake. I had it all planned out. Except for the person I'd marry. Minor detail."

Tim gives me a meaningful look. "Nicki, aren't you forgetting something?"

I set my hot dog down on the bench beside

me and put my arm around him. "You know we weren't going there, Tim. I thought you were a wonderful guy, I think for a while we loved each other, but I don't think I saw us spending the rest of our lives together, and I don't think you did either. Did you?"

"I don't know," he says softly.

"It's OK," I tell him. " 'Cause when I met Michael, nothing else mattered, nobody else. It didn't matter what some dress would be like, or the flowers. He was what was important. All of a sudden, I saw myself with this man for the rest of my life. Whatever that was."

We start eating again. The tension is broken.

"So where is Mr. Wonderful?" Tim asks, between mouthfuls.

"Back in London, I guess. I never told him about me. He really loved me, Tim. He didn't feel sorry for me."

"Nick, did you think I . . ."

"This isn't a contest, Tim. It's just what is. I couldn't hurt Michael, so I left him."

"What about him?"

"He thinks I walked out on him, and I've decided that's better than the truth, but . . ."

"But?"

"Now nothing is the same without him. But that's that." Every time I talk or think about Mi-

Liz Nickles

chael, I feel like I'm already dead. "I didn't really know him that long, but in the time we were together I guess I became dependent on him."

"You? Dependent?"

"Yeah, unbelievable as it sounds. I felt like he'd been in my life forever, or at least that he belonged there. It was just something that worked. It really worked."

"So does it have to be like this?" Tim asks. "Doesn't he get a say in this?"

"Well, it's too late now, anyway. It's over. Pass the mustard."

Even though I know he's a gutless coward, it still feels comfortable being with Tim.

He walks me back to the apartment but doesn't go in. I think he gets the drift of how Emily and Eric feel about him. It's a good thing he's so perceptive, because when I walk in, they're all over me.

"I can't believe Tim sucked you into going out with him!" Em screams.

"We did not go out. We walked maybe three feet and had a hot dog. Is that going out?"

"Well, consider the alternative," Eric says. "You could be keeping company with real human beings—like us."

"Well, everyone deserves a second chance. Even Tim. God, we were together four years."

Two days later, Tim calls again and we have breakfast. "I've been thinking about what you said," he says. "Are you sure it's over with that Michael guy?"

"Yeah, I'm sure." I stare at my fried eggs. They look like a pair of eyes, glaring up at me and calling me a liar.

"Well, I think you deserve to have love and romance in your life, Nicki. I think that was the mistake we made. We were so practical, always planning, scheduling. We never had time for romance, did we?"

"I guess not."

"Do you think if we'd had the time, things would have been different?"

Tim, Tim, Tim. We were together four years. That's enough time for an entire college education. You can learn to be a brain surgeon in four years. With Michael, it took about four seconds. But I say, "Maybe. You never know."

Tim looks at me intently, trying to read my thoughts. Fortunately, he was never good at this.

"So," he says. "You going to be around tonight?"

"Eric's cooking."

"Visitors allowed?"

"Why not?"

* * *

"I hope he's bringing a food taster," says Eric, chopping garlic with a vengeance. "You never know. I keep a messy kitchen. Rat poison could end up in his food."

"Eric, come on," I cajole.

Emily sets out place mats. She's actually wearing an apron. "Nick, if you want Tim here, we want Tim here. Right, Eric?"

Eric sighs. "You're right. Nicki, whatever you want, girl."

The truth is, it's not that I want to spend the evening with Tim, but I know how much he needs to spend it with me. He still can't forgive himself for bailing on me. I could see it in his face. Now he's trying to do anything he can to make it up to me. If he's going to live with himself, he has to. And I have to let him.

The doorbell rings.

"OK, he's here, everybody. Try to be nice, please." I stick the lettuce into the salad spinner.

Emily waves her hands and flounces to the door. "Whatever!"

Eric and I work on the garlic bread, and it's a few minutes before I realize I haven't heard a sound from the living room, and nobody's come back into the kitchen.

"Maybe she killed him?" offers Eric.

Just then, Emily sashays into the kitchen, doing her Scarlett O'Hara imitation. "Nicole, a gentleman caller."

"Tell him to come in."

"Oh, no, honey-chile. You-all're gonna wanna go out they-ah."

"Suddenly Tim can't find his way into the kitchen?" Something is going on. I go straight to the living room. Standing there is Michael. He's got his camera bag, a beat-up leather carryall, and a look on his face that makes me wonder how I could ever have spent two minutes away from him. I can't even move; I'm speechless.

Luckily, he's not. In two steps, I'm in Michael's arms. How he got here doesn't matter. I had no clue how much I missed him until this minute. The feel of him, the scent of his skin, the taste of his mouth, it all comes rushing back like a wall of water. We can't stop kissing. Eric and Emily are in the room, but we don't know it. We don't even know we're on the planet.

"Emily, do you get the feeling we're on *Melrose Place* and any minute Heather Locklear's gonna walk in?"

The doorbell rings.

"It's Heather," says Emily. She opens the door, and of course, it's Tim.

Tim takes one look and gets the picture. "Michael, I presume," he says.

"I think I just remembered, I have to practice open-heart surgery." Eric grabs Tim's arm. "You can assist."

Before Eric can hustle Tim out, Michael takes my hand and walks over to them. "Tim?" The two shake hands. Then, to my astonishment, Michael hugs Tim.

"I think I missed something here," says Emily.

But I didn't. I grab Tim. "You told him!" Somehow, he found Michael's number and called him and told him I was dying. Why else would Michael come?

Tim takes me by the elbow and leads me into the entrance hall. "I only told him one thing," he says quietly, so nobody else can hear. "That you loved him. It went down like this: Emily got his number from this Shirley person from the cruise—she's apparently phone number central—and after Em gave me his number, I called him and told him one little detail, that you loved him. That was all the man needed to hear. That's why he came. Nick, let's face reality here—it was all over your face. You never looked at me like that, you never talked about me like that. You think I don't know you? Which is also why I knew you'd never call Michael yourself. So I did it for you. And I'm not sorry."

Now it's my turn to hug Tim. "Neither am I."

He pats my back. "The rest is up to you. Tell him or not. But you know where you stand."

Now I'm scared. "God, Tim," I whisper, "I don't know if I can do this. I don't want to lose him again."

"You'll figure it out. You're the valedictorian, remember?"

Michael comes up and puts his arm around me. "Tim, thanks for the call. But I'll tell you one thing. I could never be so generous with this woman."

"Well," Tim says, serious now, "be good to her. I gotta go now. Eric needs me for his homework. Something about my aorta."

"I'm the nurse," says Emily, patting Michael's butt on her way out. "See y'all."

We're alone. Where to start? I bury my face in Michael's chest.

"So why did you run away like that, Nicki?" he asks softly. "What is it? We wasted so much time."

"I know. And I'm so sorry, but there's something we need to talk about." I force myself to take a step back and look into his eyes. "You have to listen. Now."

"What? What is all this? Nicki, there's always been something between us, something you refuse to talk about. It made you swim out to sea

177

that day, whatever it was. It made you act crazy. I thought it was another man, Tim, and I could almost understand that, but now . . ."

I put my hand over his lips. "Michael, I didn't run off that night on the boat because I wanted to leave you. I left because I had to. Because, there's something wrong with me."

He freezes. "Wrong?"

Why is this so hard to say?

"What is it? What is it, goddamn it?" Michael's voice rises with anger and concern; it feels like a slap. "What in God's name is going on here? Tell me now!"

That's it. I snap. Sobs choke out of me uncontrollably. I grab my purse, pull out my medicines in a plastic bag, and dump them on the floor at Michael's feet. "You want to know?" I scream. "You really want to know?" Before he can answer, I circle into the bathroom, shovel up a dozen more bottles of pills, run back out, and heave them onto the pile. Some of the bottles are glass, and they shatter. Others bounce or just land there like flotsam washed ashore. "Here you go, Mr. Schuster. Everything you wanted to know about Nicki, but were afraid to ask!" I am a crazy woman, a monster.

Michael says nothing, but slowly leans over, picks up a bottle, and stares at it.

I pull out drawers and wildly grab computer printouts, files, and doctors' charts. When my arms are full, I drop the pile on top of the pills. Finally, I whip an X ray of my skull out of a manila envelope and hand it to Michael. "You're a photographer. What's wrong with this picture?" I laugh bitterly, then hysterically.

All he says is, "Nicki." It's a breath.

"I'm sick. I'm dying, Michael."

He shakes his head, speechless.

"It's true." Now that I've said it, I'm suddenly overtaken by a strange calm, as if I'd taken an injection. Truth serum. "I had a relapse on the boat. That's why I left. I'm feeling better now, but it's only temporary. I don't really know how much longer I have."

"Sick? How? What's the matter? You look fine." Michael is tripping over the words.

"A brain tumor. Inoperable."

"Is this true? This can't be true!" Michael has the look of a man who has been given a death sentence himself.

We face each other now, for the first time, with all the cards on the table. "Oh, Michael, I wish to God it wasn't true, I wish we had a lifetime together. I wish I'd told you before you fell in love with me. I wish so many things, and none of them are going to happen, and I don't

Liz Nickles

blame you if you turn right around and leave."

His jaw is tight, determined. We grip each other for support. "I need to know everything," Michael says. "Because I'm going to help you fight this."

We will go to the doctor together. He will hear what I already know. And he will learn that the point is not to spend the time I have left fighting, but living. Michael will get there. I did. But the point is, when he gets there, we'll be together.

Chapter 11

*L*eaving the doctor's office with Michael, all I can think is, at least it's out in the open. I had to let him hear the whole thing from the doctor himself, and I'm relieved. There's no harder—or more heartbreaking—work than hiding something from the person you love, especially something you desperately want to share.

But even after all that's happened, I still wouldn't have blamed Michael if he'd gotten up from the chair in that doctor's office, walked out, and kept going. After all, we'd only been together in the best of circumstances, on an idyllic vacation. What we're into now is not so much the real world as the netherworld. Michael sat through it all—all the technical jargon, the prognosis zero. He looked at every X ray, every brainscan, every blood test result. It was a real trial by fire. While we were in there, Michael didn't say much, so I wondered what was going through his mind. But then, he's not the sort that so much says what he thinks as does what he feels. He's a demonstrator, a doer. Me, I'm a talker. Being with Michael makes me realize that talking doesn't change things very often—it's doing that makes a difference. Like skipping the whole part that would have involved dissecting the relationship over the phone and talking it into the ground and, instead, just getting on a plane from London and showing up on my doorstep. Like I said—doing.

Of course, I know better than anybody that the fact is, at the end of the day, there's nothing anybody can do about my situation, except be with me. But that's something, isn't it? Maybe the hardest thing. So even though things aren't any better, in a way, they are. Mom and Dad, Emily, Eric, and even Kate and Tim have been great, but that's not the same, is it? Now I have Michael's hand to hold. So I'm not alone, and it's not just that: neither is he. I think it's really more about him than it is about me. I only have to face the present: he's going to have to face the future. Alone. He has the harder job; I have to help him.

"In a way," I say as we walk to the car, his arm around me, "this is perfect."

"Perfect?"

"Not like perfect used to be, not like the way I used to think. You know what?"

"What?"

"Perfect is the time you have."

He doesn't answer. He's probably thinking, perfect in this case is pathetic, and I'd understand. But, let's face it, it's all relative.

"You know, in a way we're lucky," I explain. "We never have to worry about all the ups and downs that everybody else goes through. We're never going to fight over a mortgage. The kids are never going to keep us up at night. We're never going to grow old and fat. Like characters in a movie. The only thing is, we'll never know how it would have ended."

Michael leans over and kisses me. "I know how it ended."

"How?"

"They lived happily ever after."

The red Mustang convertible Michael rented is parked at the curb, incongruously cheerful. It is, of course, a perfect day, the kind you only see in the summer in Chicago, when the weather decides it's beaten you up enough for most of the year and will give you a sliver of a break to show you what it could be like all the time if it weren't so antagonistic. Michael walks me around and opens the door. The guy has manners, may I note? There's a side to him that's a little old-fashioned, almost courtly, which feels awfully nice to be around.

He walks back around the front of the car to his side, pausing to check something on the hood, gets in, pulls out the key, then stares through the windshield.

I reach out and touch his arm. "Michael?"

"What's that on the antenna?"

"What?"

"There's something on the antenna." He peers intently through the windshield.

"We got a ticket?"

"No, something else."

"I don't see anything."

"I see something on the antenna, Nick. I can't drive with something distracting me like that. Do me a favor? Will you get out and get it?"

I think he's lost it, but I get out of the car and peer at the antenna, wondering what it is that I'm looking for. And—damn if there isn't something on the thing. A flash of metal. Of silver. Of platinum, to be exact. Platinum, and a diamond. I can hardly believe this—it's a ring. I carefully pull it up and over the antenna and carry it back to the car.

"Is this what you were looking for?" I hold it between my thumb and second finger. It's a gorgeous diamond solitaire. The stone is not big, but it's simple, round and brilliant. Suddenly I can hardly breathe.

He takes the ring from me. "Yes, but it's not in the right place yet." He slips it on my fourth finger, left hand. "Nicole, I love you more than anything in the world and I want us to spend our lives together. Will you marry me?" He lets go of my hand, jumps up on the car seat, then kneels on it. On one knee.

I throw myself into his arms, and we roll over onto the floor of the car, between the front seat and the steering wheel. Just then, a policeman comes up and taps on the windshield as he peers in at us. "Is everything alright, miss?" he asks.

"Yes," I say between kisses. "Yes, yes, yes!"

Cruising down the Outer Drive, hugging the shore of Lake Michigan, I wave to every car that passes—with my left hand, just so I can break in the ring. Michael just happened to bring the appropriate music—a CD of "Goin' to the Chapel," which we play at top volume. And why not? Because that's where we're going—to the chapel.

Michael's on the cell phone with my dad. "So, Mr. McBain, I'm asking for your daughter's hand." Pause. "In marriage."

I will supply dialogue for my father, since I know without hearing what he's saying: "This is very sudden, Michael. Maybe we should sit down and discuss it."

"Mr. McBain . . . Dan . . . ," Michael begins.

I decide to spare him. I grab the phone out of his hand. "Dad, Michael knows everything. We just left the doctor's office. It's OK. Isn't it great? I want you to be happy for us. Will you come to the wedding and give me away?"

"And when are you planning the wedding, honey?" he asks.

"In about an hour. We're on our way to city hall right now. We called ahead. We can get the license and then get married right there."

"Right now?"

Oh, Dad. You were thinking maybe six months? "See you there."

I have a similar conversation with my mother, except she's not surprised. It turns out, she helped Michael pick out the ring this morning.

I speed-dial Emily, who leaves her job at the vet, and Eric, who manages to get somebody to cover for him in the ER. The wedding party is complete.

We pass Oak Street and are heading down
Michigan Avenue when I see it out of the corner
of my eye, as we pass the window of Saks: a
shimmering lace bridal gown—off the shoulder,
with a train. "Michael, pull over!"

"Here?"

"Right here!" He does, and I jump out of the
car. "Wait here," I command. "Don't move. I'll
be right back."

I race past a street musician playing an accordion, into the store, and ask directions to the
bridal department, never having had occasion to
be in the vicinity before. When I get there, I cor-
ral a saleswoman. "The gown in the window
with the train."

"Yes, miss?"

"Do you have it in a size six?"

She opens a notebook. "Let's see. That's a
Vera Wang. A very special dress. When is the
wedding?"

"Now."

I love the look on her face.

Fifteen minutes later, I emerge from the store
in the Vera Wang gown, the saleswoman trail-
ing behind me, holding the train and veil aloft
so they don't drag on the sidewalk. My shoulders are bare, but long illusion sleeves cover my
arms to the wrist. The dress is closely fitted to

the waist, with a row of thirty tiny satin buttons down the back. The skirt is a cumulus cloud of tulle, overdraped with lace that gathers in the back and then drops to a two-foot train. I've gathered my hair up in a loose knot at the nape of my neck, and the tulle-and-lace veil floats around my face, then swoops back behind me. With one change of clothing, I am a bride. Michael is waiting in the car at the curb, and his jaw almost hits the steering wheel when he sees me.

"Don't look!" I command. "Keep your eyes on the road! It's bad luck for the groom to see the bride before the ceremony!"

"I don't think that's a global tradition," Michael grouses, but he averts his gaze.

The saleswoman is tucking me into the car when I notice someone is in the backseat—the man with the accordion. "Excuse me?" I ask.

Michael, as ordered, stares straight ahead. "The orchestra," he explains with a grin.

The accordionist breaks into the wedding march, and we're off, my long veil flying over the backseat and the trunk.

The wedding of my dreams is nothing like the way I dreamed it would be. It's actually better. Here's what we missed: picking out a china pattern; arguing with my parents about the guest list; ordering matchbooks with our names on them. Here's what we got: everyone we care about will be there, except Michael's parents, who can't get here from Leeds in time; I have a gorgeous gown; and unlike the fifty percent of today's marriages that end in divorce, this bride and groom really will love each other until death do us part.

I admit, there are probably more picturesque places than city hall to be married—say, Positano, Italy, Paris, France, or even many dentists' offices—but to me, at this moment in time, this is the most romantic place on earth.

It's a three-step process. First, everyone we invited meets at the building entrance. Then, Michael and I get the license. Finally, we all troop to another room where the ceremony will take place. I look inside as we wait at the door for the previous wedding to end. The room itself is functional—that's about all you could say about it. But to me, it might as well be the Sistine Chapel.

The wedding party, on the other hand, is, well, vivid. My mother, of course, is crying, but, for the first time in weeks, or possibly even years, it's not because she's unhappy. Dad, Kate, and Justin are actually on time. Kate's rigged up a little sweet-smelling satin sachet pillow for Justin to carry the ring on, and Michael shows him how to stand at attention with the pillow level, so the ring won't fall off. Eric, the best man, is still in green surgical scrubs. Emily, my blue-jeaned maid of honor, has an unexpected addition to the wedding party—our wedding gift, an adorable black lab puppy she's adopted from her job at the vet whom she dubs Best Dog, but I decide to call Squirmy, because he won't stop wriggling. Mom hands me a bouquet of roses, which she proudly informs me she stole from the conservatory garden en route to city hall.

As the violinist plays a faintly recognizable Beatles medley, I go over my impromptu checklist: something new—my dress; something borrowed—the violinist; something blue—do Michael's eyes count? That leaves something old.

"Emily, you're my maid of honor. Quick! Do you have something old I can wear?"

"What a coincidence. I went by the apartment," she says, handing me a baggie. Inside are a pair of vintage lace gloves from a flea market in France, one of her most prized possessions, and my mother's charm bracelet. Perfect.

"Thanks, Em." We hug.

I pull on the gloves and turn to my mother. "Mom, would you help me with this?" When I hand her the bracelet, she smiles through her tears.

"I knew this would come in handy," she says, clipping it around my wrist. Then she holds me by the shoulders at arm's length. "My beautiful daughter." She pulls me close to her and we hold each other for a minute. Then I turn to my father and offer him my hand.

"Daddy." With that single word, our relationship is once again complete. He has his daughter back; I have my father.

Michael takes the picture.

"I guess we're ready," I announce.

"Wait!" Eric says. "I'm not dressed yet." He pulls off his scrubs to reveal a complete tuxedo underneath.

"My God, look at you!" squeals Emily.

"I always operate in black tie," he says, shrugging.

"Are you ready, Justin?" I ask my brother. "You are the most important person here. Without the ring, we can't get married."

Justin nods solemnly. "Ready," he says. He's in his Day Camp Lake Michi-Michi T-shirt, holding his arms straight out from his sides as he presents the pillow where the ring will sit for the ceremony.

"Kate, the pillow is so adorable. Thank you."

"I needlepointed it for you. It was going to be a birthday present, but I figured weddings take precedence." Kate approaches me tentatively. Even now, it's a reflex reaction—she's always wanted my approval, and she's always gotten my spite. "Nicki, I know how happy you will be. And I want you to know how sorry I am for any sadness that I've caused you by marrying your father."

"You don't have to say that," I tell her. Looking at her face, about to get married myself, I finally see who Kate really was—not a wicked conniver who stole my father, but a young woman in love who was living out her own dreams. "It's OK, Kate." We embrace, and she knows it finally really is.

The newly married couple exits the room. Our cue. Michael is on the cell phone. With who? And why now? He pulls me aside.

"My parents want to send their love to their new daughter-in-law. But why don't they tell you themselves." He hands me his cell phone, and I find myself talking to my new in-laws.

"Nicki, dear," says a lovely British voice, "Edward and I send our love to you. Michael has told us so much about you, we feel we know you already."

"I promise to take good care of your son," I tell her.

Michael takes the phone. "We have to go, Mum. We have a pressing engagement."

"We're up. Dad?" I hold out my hand. He comes to my side and offers his arm, and, to the strains of "Ode to Joy," we all walk in together.

Are your vows more heartfelt if you say them in a centuries-old cathedral, or in a garden bower, or in front of an altar than if you say them in City Hall? I think the thing that matters is your feelings for the person you're saying them to, not the place where you're saying them. As my father gives my hand to Michael, it's like an invisible thread between us, the thing that kept us connected when we were apart, suddenly contracts and pulls us even closer together, and when we say "I do," there is a seal that can never be broken, not by life, not by death.

Standing in front of the judge at City Hall, I feel that everything in my life, the terrible and the wonderful, has led me to this moment with this man. He looks at me with such love and, more than that, caring and respect. The ring and the vows we say now are superficial—we are already seared on each others' souls, we were from the minute we met. Michael looks amazing. His face, with its finely cut cheekbones and chin, is serious yet soft. His dark eyes, slightly hooded and secretive, hold no secrets for me anymore. He's wearing jeans, an open-necked shirt, and a vest, and, for once, no camera around his neck.

When it's time for the ring, Justin does his part, proudly, if precariously, presenting the little satin pillow. I lean down and give him a kiss. I want him to always remember this moment, and how important he was to it, and to me. Everyone here is important. My family.

And, most important, my husband. Michael. As we are pronounced man and wife, I hear the words, but it's more about the love that is now, officially, ours from this day till forever than the formalities of any ceremony. We hold each other and our kiss is a promise, one which can never be broken, no matter what happens tomorrow or the next day. Right now, there is no tomorrow. My cheek rests softly against his for a minute, and when I close my eyes, it's the only place on earth.

As we leave city hall, showered by rice and rose petals, still serenaded by the violinist, who, having finally figured out that Michael is British, has launched into "Rule Britannia," I notice something about Michael's Mustang. Sitting at the curb, totally illegally parked, it has morphed into a vision of wedding fantasy. White crepe paper streamers trail from every surface, and a set of corny white paper wedding bells hangs from the rearview mirror. White tissue pom-poms are planted all over the car's surface, and tin cans on strings hang from the rear bumper. Across the front of the car, a Just Married sign has been tacked to the grille. Next to this work of revisionist art, holding open the door as if he were the palace guard, stands Tim.

He shakes Michael's hand, and I kiss him on the cheek. "Be happy, Nick," he whispers.

What do you say to an ex-boyfriend who cares enough to put another man's ring on your finger? "Thank you, Tim."

For the wedding lunch, Dad offers Michael and me our choice of restaurants. Where would we like to go? We look at each other and say, in unison, "Greek."

In the car, I keep telling myself that I'm driving with my husband. I'm married. A week ago, I thought my life was over, and here it is now, just beginning. Somewhere in the pit of my stomach is a terrible fear that the headaches will return, that I will lose my sight, that the end will come. I know one day sooner than anyone should ever deserve, the inevitable awaits, like a beast in a cave, poised with a paw ready to reach out, grab me, and drag me back into the darkness. But not today. Today I am a bride. I twist the ring off my fourth finger, left hand. For the first time, I read the inscription: all the time in the world. We stop at a traffic light and kiss. All around us, horns honk at our newlywed automotive spectacle. Beautiful music.

I direct Michael to Theodora's in Greektown, your basic Greek restaurant crowded with the business lunchtime crowd, most people in suits, men in shirtsleeves with ties, jackets hung on the backs of chairs. When we walk into the restaurant, everyone freezes for a moment, forks suspended. It's probably not often a woman in full bridal regalia sweeps through these booths.

I realize when we sit down that this is going to be the first time my mother, father, Kate, Justin, and I are eating together at the same table, or eating together under any circumstances, or just doing anything together, period. Amazing. This must be what they mean by the power of love. Justin sits next to Michael and me, his new best friend Squirmy on his lap. It's hard to tell who's happier, the bride and groom, or the bride's little brother.

We order every appetizer on the menu to start and, of course, champagne. Michael and I hold hands, and I feel the pressure of a new ring, a new life. All other thoughts I push out of my mind and slam shut behind a lead-lined door, but I'm not able to block out the fact that I am so different from other brides. For them, the arc of life will lead one day—they can't possibly envision—to death. The words "till death us do part" are just words to these brides, unreal, irrelevant, a script. For me, it's all too real; but the unreal part is that the pathway to death has brought me life.

I'll settle for that.

Dad raises his glass. "To my beautiful little girl, and my new son. There is nothing more I can wish you than the love you seem to bring to each other's lives. A toast to you both . . ."

Everyone joins the toast, including Justin with his Sprite. Dad raises his glass again. "And now a toast to the other person at this table that made this wonderful day possible, because she is Nicki's mother."

"To Lori," says Kate, leading this toast, and Mom smiles softly at my father, with a look I haven't seen her give him in years: forgiveness. We are a family again.

In the car, pulling away from Theodora's with tin cans in full cry, we realize we have no plans.

Who cares? "That was the most beautiful wedding," I say.

"You are the most beautiful bride, Mrs. Schuster."

"That's Mrs. Michael Schuster to you, sir." I have to kiss him. My husband.

"So where would you like to go on your honeymoon?"

"How about something sentimental, like a cruise?"

Thirty minutes later, at sunset, we are on the deck of *The Spirit of Chicago*, the sight-seeing boat that cruises the lakefront. They don't usually take dogs, but a woman in a bridal gown can be very convincing. I decide I want to sleep in this dress. I never want to take it off. Not ever.

But, of course, I do—the minute we get to the Four Seasons Hotel, where Michael has decided to splurge on a suite. Once we're in the room and the door is closed, it takes us both about thirty seconds to get out of our clothes.

Michael takes a pink rose I saved from my bouquet and traces it along the entire length of my body, every inch. "It's like making a negative," he whispers. "Capturing an image. Your image." The petals of the rose travel down my naked hip and make soft circles on my stomach.

Then Michael slowly plucks the petals from the rose and places them, one at a time, across my breasts.

When we come together, the petals crush between us, and the sweet scent of roses is everywhere.

I am in the huge, two-person whirlpool tub, afloat in bubbles, scented bath oil, champagne, and happiness, when Michael, in a towel, comes into the marble bathroom with a cart. On the cart is a tray with plates of chocolate-covered strawberries, caviar, smoked salmon, and a large silver dome.

"Our wedding dinner," he announces, smiling. He picks up the tray, places it across the tub, and sets up his camera on the self-timer. Then he drops his towel and climbs in across the tray from me. "And no wedding dinner is complete without a wedding portrait." The camera whirrs and clicks. He refills my champagne glass and fills his own. "To the bride."

"To the groom."

We both start to laugh.

"What's hiding under here?" I pick up the silver dome. Underneath is a miniature, three-tiered chocolate wedding cake. There's even a tiny bride and groom on the top.

"This is amazing," I say. "I love it. All of it."

A silver knife festooned with white ribbons lies beside the little cake. I pick it up and try to cut through the frosting, but the knife is slippery from the bubbles and bath oil, and I manage instead to knock the cake into the tub. It goes down like the *Titanic*, with all aboard.

"Bride overboard," laughs Michael. "So much for dessert."

I fish out the waterlogged cake and give him a look. "What do you mean?" Taking a deep breath, I dive under the bubbles and the tray, emerging on his side of the tub. We are both soaked and slippery, and I slither, like a sea creature, up and over my husband. Licking the bubbles off his ear, I whisper, "Dessert is served."

Chapter 12

*M*y mom the real estate agent came through with an incredible wedding gift—the first month's rent on a one-bedroom loft in Lincoln Park. The apartment has brick walls, high, beamed ceilings, and a view of the park. It's perfect. Actually, I would rather have gone to New York with Michael and helped him get his show together, but he doesn't want to be so far from my doctors and my family. It makes him nervous. So I decided to humor him, even though I know it means I will probably never see Michael's work in a show. But I know it's the right decision. I have to get Michael set up with a support system so he's not alone when the time comes. Because I have one secret that I'm keeping from Michael, from everybody: the headaches are back. They're not excruciating—yet

—and nothing my meds can't control. But they're there, a shadow on our life, a constant reminder of the future. And I could never leave Michael in a place where he has no one to turn to.

Therefore, we are now Lincoln Park loft-dwellers. First order of married-life business: buy a bed. The loft is furnished, and it has a built-in Murphy bed, but, considering the amount of time we figure we'll be spending in the bed, that's not good enough for either of us, unless we suddenly decide to live in the wall.

Can I tell you something? One of the first things I realize after Michael and I are married is how ordinary things, like shopping for a mattress, become something wonderful and fun when you do them with someone you love. Walking the dog is an adventure with a leash. Buying groceries becomes a chance to hold hands in the proximity of produce. Picking up the cleaning is an excuse to swing by Starbucks and talk for an hour. Our life together is a series of wonderful moments, linked like the most amazing necklace by our love. We know we have to make the most of every second we have together, and we do.

So, although I can understand why some people might consider shopping for a mattress a mundane chore to check off a list, we see it differently.

As we take the escalator up to the mattress department at Marshall Field's, I have a sudden longing to get off on every floor and buy things for the apartment: sheets, spatulas, a cappuccino maker with all the bells and whistles. Yes, I know the loft came furnished, but it's not our furniture, and what I wouldn't give to decorate it my way. True, I never gave much thought to the apartment I shared with Emily, Eric, and Tim. It was just a place we passed through on our way to other things. But now it seems so important to have a home, establish a territory that's ours. I never even knew I had a domestic side, and now I want to show it to Michael.

"OK," says Michael as we head into the mattress department. "So it's in and out, right?"

"Right."

For about five minutes, we stroll through a sea of mattresses. "How do you decide on one?" Michael asks me.

"I have no clue, I guess you just pick the most comfortable one."

"How do you know which one that is? They all look alike."

A salesman in a suit approaches. You can tell that to him, all mattresses are not alike.

"We're looking for a mattress," says Michael.

"Of course. Inner spring or foam construction? Quilted top? One or five year guarantee?"

"What's the smallest bed that fits two people?" Michael asks.

The salesman smiles. "You'd want a double, or full-sized, mattress in that case."

"Double it is," I say.

The salesman lifts an eyebrow. "You'd have more room between you in a king."

"We don't want any room between us," Michael says.

"Honeymooners," I say, and I can't suppress a grin. The salesman moves on to more fruitful territory.

"So what do we do now?" Michael asks. "Every mattress in the world looks exactly alike."

"There's only one way to tell for sure: Let's give them a test drive." I take off my shoes and carefully climb onto the closest mattress, patting the surface next to me. "I saved you a place."

I have a feeling Michael is afraid we'll be arrested, but he fearlessly climbs on beside me. We lie there together, staring at the ceiling. For about two minutes. Then all hell breaks loose.

I can't help myself. I am compelled to get up and jump on the mattress.

"Nicki," says Michael disapprovingly, but I pull him up and the next thing you know, we're jumping up and down on the mattress, like little kids on recess.

The salesman rushes over. "Excuse me, that is not permitted," he says.

"We'll take it," says Michael, still jumping with me. He curtails his jumping just long enough to pick up a pillow and whack me with it. I grab it and whack back: our first fight.

On the way home, I realize that it's our one-week anniversary, so we pick up the ingredients for a special dinner. Cooking is my new thing, and I seem to have a knack for it, especially pasta. Tonight, it'll be rigatoni. We stop by Treasure Island and get garlic, fresh tomatoes, lettuce, mushrooms, and the kind of Parmesan cheese that you have to grate off the block. And wine. Especially wine.

Michael takes Squirmy for a walk and I'm stirring the sauce when the phone rings—Michael's cell, which he left on the coffee table. I drop the spoon and dive for it, but it stops ringing the minute I pick it up. There's a button to retrieve messages, so I go back to my sauce, wait a minute, and push it.

"Michael?" A female voice.

I freeze. Please don't let it be an ex-girlfriend. Or the ex-wife.

"This is Sally from New York. Sally Mortensen. Your agent, in case you've forgotten, which maybe you have, since you haven't returned my calls for over a week." Her voice sounds brisk and irritated. "I have some potential commissions for you. The creative director at Thompson loved your book, and he wants to meet you, he's talking a big fragrance shoot, on location. And the Griffon Gallery is calling. Please get back to me. These things can't wait."

I click the phone off and turn down the stove.

How selfish can I be? Sitting here in Lincoln Park focusing on mattresses and cappuccino makers while Michael's career is stuck on hold. Obviously, he didn't tell his agent anything. He just left town, and now we're married and he doesn't even live in New York anymore. I never stopped to think what marrying me would do to his career, but now it's obvious.

I hear the key in the door, and Squirmy's nails on the wood floor as Michael comes in.

"That smells incredible," he says as he unclips the leash. He deposits a bouquet of pink roses on the kitchen counter, picks up his camera, and snaps my picture.

"Michael!" He never stops taking my picture. "I'm just cooking. It's a boring picture."

"Not to me." He puts the camera down, scoops up some sauce with his finger, and licks it.

"Michael, your cell phone rang."

He unwraps the roses. "Did it?" He doesn't make a move to pick up the phone.

"You should get the message. It could be important."

"I'm on my honeymoon."

"Still." I dump more wine into the sauce. You can never have too much wine in a sauce.

"Fine. I'll pick up the message, if it'll set your mind at ease." He takes the phone and I watch him play back the message. His expression never changes. Then he puts the phone down.

"Who was it?"

"Nobody."

"It wasn't nobody."

"You're right. It was my agent, Sally."

"She has work for you."

"That's not important." He's not looking at me. I know he's lying, because I know how important his work is to him.

I set down my spoon and go over to him. "Michael, you're a brilliant photographer. Of course they want you for a job. Don't think I don't know what you're doing. But you can't turn down work because of me."

His voice is tight. "It's our honeymoon, damn it. Why can't I enjoy my honeymoon?"

"It's our life. We promised we'd live life. You

have to keep your end of the promise and not walk away from your chances like this."

"Why don't you let me be the one to evaluate my professional opportunities." He storms out of the room and I follow him.

"This isn't professional, it's personal. As personal as it gets."

"There's nothing to talk about." He goes to the window and stares out. Maybe he's wishing he could escape, live a normal life, with a normal woman. I wouldn't blame him. The poor guy can't even get mad at me without feeling guilty, like he's dumping on a dying woman. The situation sucks.

"You don't understand, Nicki, I'd have to travel."

"Then you travel. You do what you have to do. I don't need a nurse, I need a husband. Michael, I won't like having you gone, but one day I'll be the one who's gone, and if you don't have your work then, I don't know what you'll do." When Michael has his work, he's never really alone. I know that, when the time comes, it'll be his work that will see him through. "Or are you scared of something else, Michael? Of doing what you really want to do, of letting your work out into the world? Remember what I said on the boat? How long can you prepare? It's time.

I refuse to be your excuse." I put my arms around him, and we hold each other. For once, I'm the strong one, the one who gives him direction. "I married a photographer," I tell him "Go be one. Please. For me." Our arms tighten around each other.

"What if I looked for some work in town?" Michael says finally. "There's plenty of work in Chicago. I'll tell Sally that's what I want."

I kiss his cheek. "You know my closet? It is now officially your darkroom."

Let me get one thing straight. I am far from the saintly type. It kills me to tell Michael to go off on shoots, to lose him, even for a second, to his work, because every instant is so precious. But then there's reality, a monster that is always there, getting in the way of how things ought to be. Reality lives inside my head, asserting itself with every headache, with every tick of the clock. Reality, in this case, you win, but I will not leave Michael unprepared for you. I will do everything in my power to arm him against you, no matter how I feel about it.

We resolve the issue by making love in front of the window. The mattress hasn't arrived yet, it's just the bare floor, but so what. Who needs a mattress?

Chapter 13

*D*eath has a way of abbreviating things, even before it happens. When the clock is ticking, you don't want to deal with issues that are nonessential, so I've eliminated certain things from my vocabulary. Take laundry. I've never known anybody to have a meaningful relationship with a washer and drier, and I refuse to squander another second on spin cycles and stain remover. So I now send all our things out. Michael is in total agreement. In fact, he always operated this way, as a matter of course.

Another thing I've crossed off my list is the telephone. It was just eating me alive. After I started a log of my calls and discovered I spent thirty percent of my time on the phone, I decided I'd rather be experiencing, feeling, smelling, touching, than talking into a cold plastic receiver. Now, if anybody wants to talk to me, they have to do it face to face. Much better for all involved.

Also, after an entire lifetime of the calorie police, I've stopped dieting. Now I eat all the desserts on the menu. Chocolate cake, crème brûlée, banana split, chocolate-dipped strawberries, cookie plate, a sugarfest at every meal. And, as a midnight snack, the supreme no-no, Twinkies with Dove bar chasers.

Am I up at midnight? Almost always. Going to sleep is rough, even lying in Michael's arms, because sleep is time that's lost forever. The way I see it, every second that I'm asleep is one less that I have to invest in our relationship, and I'd rather spend my nights building equity. So would he. I worry about Michael being tired. I tell him to sleep, that it's OK, but if I'm awake, he refuses to close his eyes.

Which is why we're painting the apartment at two o'clock in the morning. Actually, it's a discovery: painting your apartment is the perfect activity for two o'clock in the morning because there is nothing else to do. In fact, two o'clock in the morning is the perfect time to do almost anything you can think of, because there is no competition from the world at large. Same with three o'clock, four, and even five. Six, reality begins to intrude. You are no longer alone and special: the *Today Show* people are up reporting on a weather front in Wichita.

Another thing about being up all night, or as much of it as possible—it staves off thinking. Right now, I'm not big on introspection. I don't see the point of guys like Socrates, who drink the poisoned cup of hemlock, then squander their final moments dredging down into the inner soul to haul out a riff of philosophical pronouncements that endure to stun people for centuries.

I mean, come on, people, don't you get it, you are dying, for God's sake! Think Titanic. This is not the time to rearrange the deck chairs. Every man or woman for him or herself. Focus on you. Selfish, you say? Admittedly. But here's the point: it's magic time. Time to do the impossible, to fit a lifetime into a byte. Or die trying—so to speak.

I've never really been good at painting, but I am an expert on giving directions. Michael has the roller, and he's finished two of the living room's non-brick walls. We picked our favorite color—blue, like the sky, like the ocean. It looks pretty good. I'm sitting cross-legged on the floor with a grape popsicle, and I notice a can of spray paint. Red spray paint. And inspiration strikes.

"Michael, you're doing a great job. You're a natural. But why don't you take a break and wash some of those drips off the brush," I say. "Paint's running down your arms."

"Good idea. And while I'm on my break, how would you like a pina colada?"

"Perfect idea. The blender needs exercising."

He ducks into the bathroom, and the minute I hear the water run, I jump up, grab the spray can, and spray a huge graffiti heart on the brick living room wall. Inside, I write, in script, "I love you." Just as I'm putting an arrow through the heart, Michael comes back in and busts me.

"Nicki! What . . ."

Stepping back, I survey my work. "Masterful," I proclaim.

He frowns. "Oh yeah?"

Maybe Michael is thinking about the security deposit, which we will definitely never see again, thanks to my unbridled artistic impulse. "Oh, God, Michael, I'm sorry . . ."

With a stern look, he takes the spray can out of my hand. Then he points it at the wall and sprays his own heart—bigger than mine. Inside it he paints "M.S. + N.M.S." I accept the challenge, and within half an hour, the entire brick wall is covered with graffiti hearts and kisses, and Michael and I are laughing hysterically.

"I do love you," Michael says, and we kiss, smearing ourselves with paint.

"It's not like we ruined the wall," I say. "You have to look at it as an artifact, a monument to eternal love—like the hieroglyphics and wall paintings in the pyramids."

He kisses my hair.

"Hundreds of years from now, archaeologists on a dig will unearth this wall and say, 'Two people who loved each other very much lived here.' It will become a famous wall. A tourist attraction. The Elvis of Walls."

He pulls up my paint-stained T-shirt and kisses my belly. "Tell that to the building management," or at least I think that's what Michael says as he kisses me again, this time moving downward.

I intend to. But not until I've kissed my husband back a couple of hundred times and tried out the new mattress that came today, which is now yesterday.

So when do we sleep? I admit, after the wall thing, and making love for another hour as the sun came up, we were both pretty wiped out. Somehow, when Squirmy nudged my hand to go out, it was afternoon, and I realized we had promised to meet Eric, Emily, and a few of their friends for dinner in just two hours. Chinese.

"Sure you want to go?" Michael asks, rolling himself deeper into the sheet as Squirmy scrambles onto the bed.

"Yeah, I really miss those guys."

He fakes looking hurt. "Oh, I'm not a fit replacement, then? Should we ask them to move in?"

"Well, maybe I don't miss them that much. It's kind of fun to be able to walk around naked." I lie still and close my eyes. There's something going on in my head, very far away, and I want to keep it there, at bay. I will ignore it, get up and put on my red Chinese-style dress, the skintight one with the thigh-high slit that Emily forced me to buy and I never wore before. It's funny. Now that she's training to be a vet, Emily's dressing in chinos, white shirts, ponytails, headbands: Ralph Lauren meets Soccer Mom. And I'm the one who's become partial to costumes. Suddenly, I'm into making a statement. Like the writing on the wall, I want to be remembered. Actually, I insist on it. So I'm into dangly earrings, clothes that show my shape, teetery platforms. I've developed what the magazines call a "signature scent," a jasmine bath oil that I dab at my elbows, knees, and throat. At the first whiff, Michael becomes unhinged, and the scent of jasmine lingers behind on our sheets, and hangs in the air after I've left a room, so I'm there even when I'm not. I apply blood red lipstick with a brush. Look in the mirror, Nicole. Do you like what you see? A woman, a lover, a wife.

Michael bites the bullet and drags himself out of bed to walk Squirmy. I lie there, waiting, until I hear the door close. Then I'm up and into the bathroom. My brushes, bottles, and beauty potions are stacked in baskets on the vanity, but I head for the medicine cabinet. My pills. My meds. I'm like the lady heading for the roulette table at Las Vegas. Where will the little ball drop tonight? Red or black? Freedom or death? I gulp my pills, drop back onto the bed, and hold my breath, willing them to work.

The key in the door; Michael is back.

"Nick?" He comes into the room. "What a cheat! You never got up. Well, two can play that game." He flops down beside me. "So, changed your mind? Want to stay in?"

I reach out for him. "Let's split the difference. We'll miss the appetizers."

An hour later, we finally get to Dee's, my favorite Chinese place. "This isn't very polite," I whisper as we make our way to the table. "What are they going to think?"

"Nothing at all," says Michael breezily. "We're

a bit late, so that's all there is to it. Unavoidably detained."

Emily, Eric, and two guys I don't know are holding down the table. Emily takes one look at us and gives me an eyebrow that says "I know what you've been up to." She always knows. She's psychic that way, when sex is involved.

"Meet Dr. Jim Anders and Dr. Jay Steinberg," Em says, indicating the men sitting on either side of her. One of them looks about eighteen years old. I wouldn't want him operating on me. We all shake hands, and I slide into the booth, Michael opposite me.

"We're having champagne," says Emily, waving her hand, and I know it's because it's my favorite drink, but tonight I can't have any. I've taken too much medicine.

"Pass, thanks," I say, leaning to kiss Emily as Michael snaps a shot of us.

"Jimmy was just telling us about this bitch he saved," Em says, obviously infatuated. She can't take her eyes off this guy who saves people, even though they're bitches. He's red-haired, baby-faced, freckled, glasses, in some circles would be considered an underage geek. Not her usual type, but clearly Emily sees something in him. I wonder what.

"Well, she's a Doberman, and she's just delivered ten pups," Jim begins, as Emily leans in to catch every word.

Oh. That's what.

"Listen to this," Emily interrupts. "He saved them all! It was incredible!"

"No, you were incredible," he says, shaking his head. "You knew just what to do, and you never panicked. You're a natural, you know that?"

"Get out!" Emily beams. It was worth going out tonight just to see this. Somehow I don't think we need to worry about Emily anymore. These two were made for each other.

Eric gets it, too. "Well, excuse me, but Jay here operated today, too, and his patient was a real bitch, walking around, two-legged variety on her third face-lift."

"I took off ten years," says Dr. Jay. "She loves me."

"I assisted," Eric informs us. "My first face-lift."

"You were wonderful," says Jay, "although you may have pushed the envelope a bit when you told her she looked exactly like Melanie Griffith."

"Please, Jay. The woman's from Beverly Hills. It's the ultimate compliment."

"Eric, she's seventy. Tippi Hedren, at the most."

"You are incorrigible."

"Soulmates," whispers Michael. "We should have stayed at home. These guys don't need us."

"Waiter, more steamed vegetable dumplings," says Emily.

"What do you feel like, Nicki?"

I'm not hungry, but I say, "Egg drop soup."

"Nick, that's not food, you can't even eat it with chopsticks. What else?"

"That's it. Really. Now tell me more about the Doberman."

The courses keep coming, and Michael gets into the story of our motorbike ride in Greece.

"You should have seen the two of them on the motorcycle," says Emily. "It was hysterical."

"What do you mean!" Michael is indignant. "I was Evel Knievel."

"What do you mean?" I interrupt. "You were pathetic. I, on the other hand, was brilliant."

"I thought I drove. You mean, you were a brilliant backseat driver. Pass the rice."

By the time the third dish comes to the table, the conversation seems to whirl around me, like a brewing storm. It's suddenly too much effort to keep up, so I sit back and just try to listen.

Michael notices. "Nick?" He leans across the table.

I don't want to leave, but I can't deny it anymore. The headache. Like a sledgehammer that obliterates a wall from the inside out, it's broken through the shell of my skull and is throbbing relentlessly. The pills are either wearing off, or they didn't ever really work. It's hard to tell which, but it doesn't matter. "Home," I telegraph to Michael. We don't need to talk.

"Excuse me, everybody, but I forgot to tell Nicki that I have a shoot tomorrow at dawn, so if you don't mind, we'll be cutting out a bit early," Michael announces, standing up. He knows that if he says I don't feel well, they'll swarm me—the doctor and the vet—and I'm likely to end up with a nose job and a distemper shot. There's a lot of dissension, but the fact is, this group is pretty self-sustaining without us. We escape.

"What is it, Nick?" Michael asks the minute we're out of earshot. "Should I call the doctor?"

Just saying the word *doctor* puts a tinge of panic in Michael's voice, and I hate that. "No doctors. I'm just tired. A little rest, and I'll be fine."

If only that were true, but I squeeze Michael's hand.

Chapter 14

*H*ere's my recipe for chicken salad: Get one whole carryout roasted chicken. Strip off the skin. Give the skin to the dog, but never the bones, which could splinter and be harmful (this from Emily). Then pull the meat from the bones and shred it into one-inch pieces. Take one ripe mango, skin and cube. Toss with the chicken and one eight-ounce container of plain, lowfat yogurt. Add one chopped scallion and one-half teaspoon of curry powder. Stir with a fork. Serve on leaf lettuce, never iceberg. What I like about this recipe is it is cooking that involves nothing except carrying out, shredding, cutting, and stirring. Even I can do it.

Wait a minute. Didn't I swear off cooking forever? Yes, but then I decided Michael deserved something special, and this is something I can actually do. Believe me, even when your head is pounding off your shoulders, you can still stir. The other thing is, I'm finding, after years of charging toward big goals, that the little things are a more major part of life than I ever gave them credit for. Someone, I forget who, once said, "Life is what happens while you're making other plans." And it's true.

While I'm skinning the chicken, the phone rings.

"Hello?"

"Hello, I'm trying to reach Nicole McBain."

I can't place the voice, but obviously the man doesn't know I'm now Nicole Schuster. "This is Nicole." I wipe my greasy hands on a towel. "Who's this?"

"Arnold Gardener."

"Of Avery, Gardener and Brown?"

"None other."

"This—this is Nicole." I still remember my interview with Mr. Gardener, and, verbatim, the conversation in which he offered me the internship.

After I was in the hospital, I wrote him a letter, turning it down.

"Nicole, we've been trying to get in touch with you, but your number was disconnected."

"Yes, Mr. Gardener, I got married and moved."

"Well, congratulations. Actually, I called Northwestern, and the alumni office gave me your new phone number. I hope you don't mind."

"No, I don't mind."

"Well, the reason I'm calling is that we of course received your letter and, to be frank, I wanted to try to change your mind. Have you accepted something with another firm?"

"No, it's not that, Mr. Gardener."

"I understand. You had a wedding to attend to. My own daughter got married last year. The household was in an uproar for six months. My wife still hasn't recovered. Well, the intern we ended up hiring has not worked out, so the position is vacant, and we were wondering if you'd be able to join us at this time. I want you to know, Janet Avery is bound and determined to have you on our team. She has a special assignment from the Department of the Interior that we think you'd find very challenging."

I want to jump through that phone and say yes. I want to hug Mr. Gardener, kiss him on top of his comb-over head. I want to put on a business suit and take the 157 bus straight down to Michigan and Congress and assume my rightful place on that team. Damn it, I worked so hard for it; I earned it; it's mine. Tears splash onto the roast chicken. What recipe calls for tears?

But instead, I say, "Mr. Gardener, thank you so much. You don't know what this means to me. And I'm so sorry I didn't call you personally before. I just thought a letter would be best. You see, I just can't take a job at this time."

"Well, Nicole, all I can say is, your feelings are not uncommon. My daughter felt the same way when she was a newlywed, but, you know, after a few months, she was ready to go back to work, and now she's teaching. We respect your wishes, of course, but if I may say something here, Nicole, of all the interns I have met over the years, you were the most perfect fit for this firm. I honestly felt you thought so yourself. Well, perhaps you'll feel differently in the fall. The door is open."

No, Mr. Gardener, the door is closed. Or, let's be more accurate: it slammed shut on me.

Because I will never have a whole life. My life is like this chicken: picked nearly clean. I'm living on the morsels that are left, hoping they will last just a little longer.

"Thank you, sir," I whisper, and manage to hang up without crying. I stand there for a long time, staring at the kitchen counter, willing the chicken and the mango to turn themselves into a salad on their own.

I'm thinking that the call from Mr. Gardener was depressing when something else happens that catches me totally off guard.

It starts with a walk in the park, a hot summer day. Michael's on a shoot, and I'm walking Squirmy in Lincoln Park, the part with the Farm in the Zoo. Suddenly, Squirmy spies an approaching stroller and leaps up to make friends with its occupant, whom he no doubt sees as a peer. Down reaches a tiny hand, up slurps Squirmy's tongue, and a bond is forged.

"What a cute puppy," says the baby's mother.

"And she's adorable," I say politely, smiling sociably in the direction of the child.

The little girl leans over, and her hat falls off, onto the pavement. I quickly lean down to pick it up. The moment the hat touches my hand, my knees go weak. It's the cutest, littlest hat I've ever seen, pale pink with black and white sheep crocheted in a pattern. The yarn feels soft, like angora. I carefully place the hat back on the little girl's head. Her silky blonde hair brushes my fingers. Leaning over her, I can smell her baby scent.

"Let's go, Squirmy," I say, yanking the leash. Our departure is abrupt.

So that was it. The baby that will never be mine. Will never be ours. I'll never know if our child would have Michael's eyes and my nose, or vice versa. If she'd have musical talent, or be good at soccer. Or if she'd even be a she.

This is the worst of all, especially since I never thought I wanted children, and I am so totally unprepared for this naked, aching baby lust.

Then it hits me. I never wanted a child because I wasn't married to Michael. Being married to him, it's the most natural thing in the world to want a family. To know that if not now, someday, when the time was right, it would happen.

How flip I've been to say that we're lucky not to ever be woken up at 2 A.M. by a crying baby. How easily I shrugged off changing diapers.

I will never have a child. That's a fact. Michael may, someday, with another woman. That's another fact, perhaps the most painful. How can I let some other woman have Michael's child? I walk for awhile and mull over how I'd feel about Michael with another woman. It's not pretty. But do I want Michael to someday see a baby and realize that will never be part of his life? Do I want him to feel this pain I'm feeling now?

No. Never.

So I will pray, with all my heart, that Michael

will find love again, marry, and have the child he deserves. And, if he balks, I plan to kick his butt from heaven, if necessary. If it's the last thing I do.

Chapter 15

This morning, when I open my eyes, Michael brings me a breakfast tray, but there isn't any breakfast on it. "Happy fourth anniversary," he says, putting the tray on the bed beside me. Squirmy jumps up alongside in search of non-existent bacon, and I tuck him in with me. Michael picks up his camera and takes my picture with the dog under the covers. "I love the way you two look in bed."

We've been married four weeks. An entire month. We are now an old married couple. On the tray is a large, beautiful, rectangular box covered in pale lavender linen. Carefully, I lift the lid. There's a layer of a kind of parchmenty paper, and beneath it, I discover a stack of beautifully mounted photographs. The first one is of me. So is the second. They all are.

"These are gorgeous, Michael. Except for the subject."

"What do you mean? You are gorgeous. Can't you see?" He takes the stack of pictures and props them up, one at a time, all over the room. Here I am on the deck of the *Circe*, sun spangling the water in the distance. Here I am in the Temple of Aphrodite, blowing a kiss. Here I am poised at the edge of a cliff, wind whipping my hair, arms stretched toward the sky, ready to jump.

There's a slight blur around the edge of each image of me, as if I'm in motion, going somewhere fast. "I tried some new tricks with the exposures and filters," Michael says. "I like what's happening in these pictures. There's a Man Ray kind of feeling."

"And the subject?"

"I love the subject."

"I have an anniversary present for you, too."

"What?"

"Squirmy's housebroken. We finally did it."

"One month," says Michael, and he leans over the bed and kisses me softly. The words hang in the air. For us, every day is an achievement, but also a loss. A calendar page ripped off and gone forever, leading to the end. The longer we've been together, the less there is to celebrate, really. But we love to celebrate, so we have more reasons than anybody: the four-week anniversary of our wedding; the two-month anniversary of our meeting; the thirty-day anniversary of when we said we loved each other; Squirmy's rabies shot anniversary; you name it, we'll celebrate it. Michael and I have winter birthdays, so we've had two un-birthdays, just so we could have cakes and blow out the candles and sing "Happy Birthday" to each other.

For our first-week anniversary, Michael gave me an antique, heart-shaped locket set with amethysts, my birthstone. I never take it off. I gave him a book on Alfred Stieglitz, one of his photography heroes. On our second-week anniversary, I surprised Michael with tickets to an outdoor concert in the suburbs, at Ravinia, where we sat outside on the lawn, set candles and a bottle of wine on a blanket, and listened to Beethoven under the stars. Michael gave me a huge gardenia plant, with dozens of blooms that make the loft smell like a garden. Then, on our third-week anniversary, he gave me a huge wrapped box with a pink bow, and inside it was another wrapped box with a yellow bow, then a box with a peach bow inside that, and so on, until the very last box, which was smaller than the palm of my hand, and inside was a comb for my hair, decorated with the tiniest, most beautiful shells in sunset colors. I gave him a watercolor of a beach that reminded me of Greece. But, mostly, what we give each other is love.

I once saw a TV interview with a famous Grand Prix race car driver. The interviewer asked him the secret to his success. He said that, to the average person, it seemed as if the cars in the race were moving at a blazing speed. But, to him, time slowed down when he was in a race. An everyday second was his hour, a minute was forever. He was aware of every portion of every second, and each fraction of time was, to him, a leisurely experience, allowing him to master the moment and stretch out the time he had. It's like that with us. However much time we have, it's a lifetime.

Michael sits on the edge of the bed. "Want to go out for breakfast?"

"Nope."

"How about one of my killer omelettes?"

"Mmm. But I'm just not hungry."

He shifts his posture, just enough that I know he is on alert. "Why?"

"No reason."

"Headache?"

"Ummm . . ." I can't lie to Michael about this ever again.

"Look at me."

I'm flooded with a wave of relief, because now I have someone to share this with. I would never have told Michael; but he sensed it, of course. Probably he's known from the very beginning. Have we both been in denial? Then again, don't tell me denial isn't preferable.

Michael's lips tighten so subtly that nobody but me would have noticed. He moves the box and the tray and lies down beside me, holding my hand. Our chests rise and fall as we breathe in synch. "So what would you like to do?" he asks.

I'm no fool. I know he expects me to say something like get a blood test or another head zap, but I surprise him. "Go to Six Flags," I say.

"What exactly is a Six Flags?"

"It's an amusement park. You know—as in rides, roller coasters, cotton candy."

"Roller coasters?"

"You chicken?" I elbow him in the side.

"Ouch! Of course not!"

"Vertigo?"

"Me?"

"So let's go. That's what I want to do for our anniversary."

He squeezes my hand. "Nick, are you sure? Is it a good idea for you to go on a roller coaster?"

"Going on a roller coaster is not going to make my health worse or better. It'll just make me feel better. Especially with you. In America, you have to go to the amusement park with your husband. It's a tradition."

He gives me a look.

"Well, it's our tradition. As of now. And let's bring Justin. If we call Kate right now, maybe she'll let us take him along." Suddenly, I desperately want to go on the roller coaster. I want to be normal, not sick.

Walking into Six Flags, we could be any all-American family—the woman, the man, the little kid in the baseball cap, all heading for a day of fun.

Justin goes wild immediately, wanting to go on every ride in the park: Batman, The Riddler, Superman, rides that would freeze any sensible adult to their seat.

"This is great, Nicki!" he yells, tugging my hand.

"Not better than the wedding!" I pretend to be horrified.

"Well . . . maybe," he says happily. No guilt there.

We stand in line and get sno-cones, popcorn, hot dogs, every kind of junk food.

"Wow!" squeals Justin. "My mom never lets me eat this stuff."

"It's our secret then, buddy," winks Michael. Out of the corner of his eye, he looks at me, and I know he's watching to see how I feel.

My goal: not to let him know.

One thing about a headache, when you're on a roller coaster, you have other things to think about. Justin and I go together on the Bat Challenge, Michael behind us. We can't go on the biggest roller coaster, because Justin is too little.

It doesn't matter. No roller coaster could be as terrific as watching Justin's face. The roller coaster creeps up, dives down, whiplashes around, and we scream and hang on to each other. When it finally slows down, I think, this is like my life. I wonder what it would be like if they made a ride out of my life? Nicki's Nemesis. Actually, here's what I think: if my life were a ride, they'd have to pull it from the park. There'd be too many complaints. Too scary. Too heavy on the shock value. Worst of all, too short. Everybody would demand their money back. Well, I'm stuck with it, but Michael and Justin are part of it, so I wouldn't trade.

*   *   *

Back at the loft, Michael takes Squirmy for his walk, and I take some more of my meds. I'm headed for the kitchen when it's like somebody turned out all the lights. I know what's happening. I wish I didn't know.

The first thing is not to panic. Panicking did not help before, so there's no point in going through that again. Feeling with my hands, I make my way into the living room area, find the couch, and sit down. And wait.

I hear the door open, Michael unclipping Squirmy's leash and dropping it on the counter. His footsteps on the wood floor. The refrigerator door open.

"Can you think about dinner, Nick?" he says. "You wanted to make pasta."

"Not tonight, if that's OK. Would you mind ordering out?" My voice sounds perfectly normal. Of course, so do the voices of lunatics, sometimes.

"What are you doing sitting here in the dark?"

I hear the lights click on. Was it dark? God, I didn't even know. That's it. My personal monster is back, and it's grabbed me and dragged me into that awful place where there's no way out. But there's always the chance for a reprieve. It wouldn't be the first time, would it?

"There," says Michael. "That'll put a little

light on the subject. Now. What about Thai?"

I realize I can't stay on the couch forever. I stand up and walk toward the sound of Michael's voice. My foot stubs into something soft but sturdy, and Squirmy yelps as I stumble.

"Nick!" Michael grabs me, steadies my arm, and pulls me close.

"I'm sorry, Squirmy," I say. "Good dog." I reach for him, stretching out my fingers.

"Squirmy's fine, Nicki," Michael says quietly, taking my hand and holding it, then placing it on Squirmy's soft back. "But are we? We can't pretend nothing's happening."

His chest feels so good. "We're not. I just wish it wasn't, that's all. But if it has to happen, we're together."

"So what now?" he asks, stroking my hair.

"You know how our marriage vows said 'For better, for worse'?"

"Of course."

"Well, I guess this is what they meant."

Chapter 16

I'm sitting in yet another specialist's office for one reason only: Michael. It's not fair to let him handle everything without anybody advising him except me. And he still has hope, in spite of everything, that things will get better. I suppose he has to believe that—but I have to deal with what's going on inside my head. So does Dr. Graham. I hear his chair scrape closer to the desk, papers rattle. Michael grips my hand, his thumb stroking my wrist. My mother and father are here, too, flanking us. I can smell Mom's perfume. Coco.

"The fact that she's lost her vision again tells us that her condition is advancing to another stage," says Dr. Graham. "But we don't know for sure. If she were in the hospital, we could perform some tests . . ."

"Forget the hospital," I cut him off. "And I'm sitting right here, Doctor, you don't need to talk about me as if I'm not in the room. Tell me, if you put me in the hospital, can you make me better?"

"I don't think so, Nicole. We can treat, but not cure, your condition."

I gulp. OK, I remind myself. This is nothing new. You can handle it. "What can you do for me, without the hospital?"

"Well, we can certainly make you as comfortable as possible."

"That's it?" My stomach tightens. Please say there's something else. This can't be it. "Can't I get my sight back? Up my meds?"

"If it does come back, Nicki, it will only be temporary. I wish the news was better, but I know you want the facts."

Do I? Maybe I'd rather be in denial, but what good would that do Michael?

"It varies from individual to individual. There are exceptions—in some cases, patients with NF2 can exist with the condition for years before neurological symptoms develop. You're exhibiting symptoms now, as you know, and they are intensifying. Still, there is always a chance that the tumor development will arrest, although that is very rare. We could perform surgery . . ."

"But would that cure me?"

"Not cure, no. And it is highly risky."

"Then what's the point? No surgery."

"I fight with myself on this every day, Doctor," Dad interrupts. "If it were up to me, I'd get her to a hospital this minute."

I turn to the sound of his voice. "Oh, Dad. I know it's hard. But I've faced it, Michael's faced it, now you have to face it, too." I'm sure my mother is crying. "Mom, you need to hear this, too. Here are the facts. I'm blind. I'm not getting better."

"Honey . . ."

"Please, Mom. That's just the way it is. I'm blind but guess what? I'm still here. I have a husband and a marriage and a family and I want to enjoy them for as long as I can. Say what you will about hospitals, there is nothing there to enjoy. So, Doctor, while we're facing facts here, I'm not into pain. I'm ready for the bigtime pain setup at home. That sounds like the right next step. Can you help us with that? And set up some help for Michael?"

"Michael," says Dad, "are you going to let her do this?"

"I don't 'let' Nicki 'do' anything, Dan. She makes her own decisions, and I support them. If this is what Nicki wants, to handle things at

home, then as far as I'm concerned, that's it."
Michael's voice is even but firm. "I'm here to
support her all the way. She knows that."

"And what about you, Michael?" asks the
doctor.

"Me. Well, I'm hardly the issue."

"But you are part of the issue. The burden is
on you."

"Nicki is never a burden. Anything but. She's
so much stronger than me, than any of us."

"Maybe you could help Michael. Tell him
what to expect," I say.

"You're not alone, Michael," says Mom.
"We're a family here. And Nicki needs you."

Michael's voice is shaking. "I can handle that.
What I can't handle is how much I need her. I
always thought I was so independent. Didn't
need anyone for anything."

I'm out of my chair and wrapping him in my
arms. This is more painful than anything my
health could bring me. "Michael, I'm so sorry,"
I whisper.

"How can I help you, if I can't deal with this
myself?" he says, and I wipe away his tears.

"We'll help each other," I say.

In a lot of ways, the person who is dying has
it easier than anybody else. You have no choices,

your course is set and finalized, while everybody around you is wondering if they're doing the right thing. The thought occurs to me—maybe I was selfish marrying Michael. The reality of how this is for him is so hard for me to take. Yes, we are entering a new stage in our relationship. Up till now, Michael has been there for me. Now, I will have to be there for him.

If the situation were reversed, I can't imagine how I'd feel. Losing Michael would kill me. I'd rather lose myself than my love. Isn't it funny? I'm going to get my wish.

Now that I can't see, I have to force myself to admit that we'll need help. Here are the facts: maybe I'll get my sight back, maybe not. Worst-case scenario, I know there are many people who are blind and function with perfect independence. But I'm not sure that I'm as brave as they are. This is definitely not going to be a piece of cake.

We go home, and the rest of the group comes along. We need a family conference. Dad offers to come by after work. Mom will take a leave of absence and help with meals. Kate will buy groceries and supplies. The main thing is to let us enjoy our time together, not turn Michael into a nurse, which I'd hate. He's my husband, and that's his part in all this. Our goal is to keep some semblance of a life together in the midst of chaos.

"There's a lot I can still do," I remind everybody. "Walk the dog with Michael. Talk. Go out. Listen to music. Play with Justin. Have a picnic. Go to a concert. So I'll give up embroidery and miniature-painting. Tough break." There's a bit of laughter, so I force myself to smile. You have to keep your sense of humor, even when things are not the slightest bit funny.

"Dr. Graham is arranging for a visiting nurse to handle the medications," says Michael. "But until we need it, Nick and I will manage."

I want to thank them all for being here for me, for their love and support—but don't you think it sounds too much like a farewell speech, totally melodramatic? Besides, they know how I feel. So I guess we'll just get on with it, this business of living and dying. Just like everybody else, except my timing is a bit off. Kisses, hugs, more tears, and, finally, everybody leaves, and I realize I'm exhausted.

"Do you want to go to bed, Nick?" Michael asks.

"No. Let's stay here, in the living room. But I'd like to lie down."

I feel Michael slipping my shoes off, and he

gently rubs my feet, toes first, then the arches and ankles.

"Are you OK?" I ask him. What I wouldn't give to see his face, but of course every feature is clear in my mind. I know that his chin is set and firm, refusing to give in to anything that could erode our relationship; his upper lip is curved and soft and gentle as ever; his eyes flicker over my face like a searchlight, missing nothing, ever. Knowing this makes it somehow easier not to see it.

"Not really. I suppose we'll just take one day at a time. Every day is like a wedding gift." He pulls my dress over my head, then gently covers me with the quilt we keep draped over the couch.

"I came back before," I remind Michael. "I can do it again."

He tucks the blanket around me and helps me lie down on the couch. "Yes you can, Nicki. You will."

"Let's stay here all night. I feel like an invalid in bed."

"Fine," he says. "We'll both sleep here. Just don't hog the couch and snore in my ear." He squeezes onto the couch beside me.

"Much better than the bed," I say. "And I don't care if you snore."

We fall asleep in each other's arms.

* * *

When I wake up, I have no idea what time it is. Not being able to see is totally disorienting, especially if you haven't had time to learn how to compensate. When I sleep, I feel like I can see, and it's such a shock to open my eyes and find that I can't. The first instant after I wake up this morning, I think my blindness is part of a dream. When I realize it's not, I nudge Michael. "Are you awake?" I whisper, hoping he is.

"Uh-huh," he mumbles. He's clearly still sleeping.

"What time is it?"

"Four A.M." He stretches.

"What do you do at 4 A.M.?"

"Go back to sleep."

"What else?"

"Guess."

And that's when I find out something amazing. Just feeling Michael is every bit as exciting to me as seeing him. Under the quilt on our couch inside our apartment, I am protected and loved. Here, nothing can go wrong. I am not sick; I am strong. I am not dying; I am living. For as long as we are here, together, I draw strength from Michael's body, and I have it all. Nobody can tell me otherwise.

Chapter 17

I refuse to go to the hospital, so the hospital comes to me: oxygen mask and tanks; bedpans; blood tests administered by visiting nurses; an IV drip for pain.

Dying happens so fast, once it starts. It's like a flood, where the water begins as a trickle and then rushes toward the dam, which can hold it back for only so long. At first, there are the tiniest of hairline cracks and leaks, and then the whole dam goes. And where you are or who you are doesn't matter.

There are a few things I'm insisting on—candles with a lemon scent, music at all times, and Squirmy at the foot of my bed. And forget the hospital gown. Emily is my fashion consultant, and she's brought me some great Chinese silk robes, which I wear all the time. I love the way they feel against my bare skin, like cool liquid.

Everybody drops by all the time. My family, of course, and Eric, Emily, and Tim. Emily is usually with Jim Anders, which is the best thing that could possibly happen. Just from the light in their voices, I know Emily and Jim are in love. I wish I could be there to share it with her. One of the worst parts about dying is knowing you're not going to be able to do the things you take for granted when you're not. I think Emily's going to marry Jim eventually, and I long to be a part of it. Then, one day when she's stopped by with a new velvet pillow for me, I realize that I *can* be a part of it.

"Em, can I ask you something?"

"Sure, Nick." She tucks the pillow next to my cheek, where it feels as luscious as a ripe peach.

"Are you and Jim getting serious?"

"I don't know. Maybe. I really am crazy about him."

I smile at that one. "Really?"

"Yeah, imagine that. Me, serious."

"So will you do me a huge favor?"

"Name it, girlfriend."

"In my closet, at the far end, is something I'd like you to have."

She slides open the closet door, and I hear hangers clattering as she rifles the clothes hanging on the pole.

"Look in the zipper bag."

I hear it unzip, then a gasp. "Oh my God, this is your wedding dress, Nick."

"Right. So it is. When the time comes, Em, will you wear it, please? For me? You can feel free to make any alterations or changes you want. Make it yours, but will you wear it?"

Emily squeezes onto the bed beside me. "Nicki, I'd be so happy to wear your wedding dress. If he ever asks, that is. I bet if I was a German shepherd, he'd already have popped the question."

We both start laughing, and it feels great.

"But you'll be at my wedding, Nick," Emily says.

"I will, I promise." One way or another.

As the days pass and I feel less strong, it's getting harder and harder to be social, but I feel like I have to try for my family. Existing takes so much energy. It's easier to keep your eyes closed, give in to the pain medications, and float, but to do that would be cheating people who love me, so I resist the temptation as much as I can.

I feel a hand on my forehead—my mother.

"Hi, honey. I'm here. With your dad."

Their voices sound so calm that I have to

smile. "So this is what it took to get you guys back together." With them side by side by my bed, I feel like a little girl again, tucked in, with the lights just out before I go to sleep. In a strange way, I think Mom and Dad feel better, too. Taking care of me is something they can do; it makes them feel like they're helping me.

"You know, guys...," I say as Mom pours me a glass of water and Dad is reading me the business section of the *Chicago Tribune* aloud. I don't care about business anymore, but it makes Dad happy to do it.

"What is it, honey?" asks Dad, pausing from his reading.

I want to tell them that even when things were at their worst between us, I always loved them. I want to—but I can't. It seems so final to say words like that. Things may be final, but I don't want to act like they are. Besides, I know they understand that I loved them. They're parents.

As for Michael, we don't have to talk at all. I sense his presence in the room, I hear his words before he says them. A touch between us is a conversation. Michael is like my coach. He gives me the motivation to make it through another day, even though I know he must be dying inside himself. But he never lets on. Since the doctor's office, he's come to terms with things. We're not trying to be strong for each other; we *are* strong for each other.

Should I tell everyone that I feel myself winding down? That it's almost like I have to force my heart to beat? Maybe they realize it already. But, at the end of the day, it's all about quality, not quantity. And when it comes to quality, I've had more than a lifetime's worth, haven't I?

The one exception is Justin. He is my biggest regret. For so long, I cheated him of a sister, and myself of a brother.

"Justin is so cute," says Mom as she straightens the covers. "He's out there with Kate teaching the puppy tricks."

The puppy. "Michael?"

"Yes, Nick?"

"Do you think we should lend Squirmy to Justin? Then maybe he won't be sad."

"Yes, I think that's a good idea. I'll get Justin, so you can tell him."

A minute later, I hear Justin come up to the side of the bed, his little feet shuffling.

"Jus, do you think you could do me a big favor?"

"What is it?"

"Take care of Squirmy for a while. He needs somebody to run and play with him, somebody closer to his own age. Like you." I squeeze his small hand. "Right, Michael?"

"Right. After all, you guys are great friends."

"Will you take him home with you, please, Justin?"

"Can I?"

"If you promise to love him."

"I promise. Thanks!" He plants a wet kiss on my cheek.

Suddenly it's hard to breathe. A struggle.

"Maybe you and your mom could take Squirmy for a walk outside now," Michael says.

"Are you OK, honey?" asks Mom.

I try to nod. "Remember, Dad," I say. "You have two sons now, right?"

"Right," he says. "You rest." He and Mom leave the room.

Something is different, but I don't want them to know. For the first time, I feel like I am losing. Death is breathing in my face. "Michael! I love you. I don't want to leave you."

"You won't, Nick. We'll always be together."

"I love you, Michael," I whisper. Everything seems to be getting farther and farther away, as if my life were at one end of a long tunnel and I were at the other, watching from a distance that is gaining on me, every second now.

"And I'll never stop loving you, Nick," Michael says, lying beside me now, stroking my hair.

He knows.

"What do you see? Look, we're lying together in the sand. Feel the sun on us—do you feel how warm it is?"

I try.

"The sky is clear sapphire blue," Michael says. "We're on a cliff, remember it? We're high above the ocean. Come on now, take my hand."

He wraps his hand around mine, ignoring the IV line. "We're going to jump together. We've done it before. You can do it. You're not afraid. You're going with me, right?"

I can only squeeze so slightly.

"Together," he says. "I'll never leave you."

I see it now, the clear blue of the water and sky. Of eternity. Once again, I have Michael's hand.

I can do this.

I jump, weightless. I fly.

Chapter 18

*H*ere's what I think about funerals: people should have them while they're still alive. Why should you have to wait until you're dead to hear all the people you know stand up and say nice things about you? And once you're dead, people have a hard time having fun, no matter how nice the funeral is.

For instance, Michael's parents have come over for my funeral. I certainly would have preferred to meet them under better circumstances, as you can imagine.

Then there's Emily. It would not be unthinkable for Em to turn up in full mourning regalia, including a black veil, but she's got on a basic black pantsuit, no makeup—or else the kind that takes three hours to look like nothing—and she's with Jim Anders. I suspect she will be with him for a very long time. She gets up to speak first.

"My best friend Nicole always did everything before anybody else," Em says. "She was first in her class, the first one to get early acceptance at school, the first one of us to get a real job, the first one to fall in love and the first one to get married. Now, she is the first one to die, and none of us know how we will get along without our beautiful Nicole. But, Nicki, we know you will get along without us, because you have always forged your own trail, made your own way. And although your life was shorter than it ever should have been, you had things and did things that many of us will never do, no matter how long we live. You showed us, Nick, that life is not about quantity, but quality. You had a life of the highest quality, Nicki, and we are so glad we were there to share it with you, for however long." Emily bites her lip and steps away.

Eric is next. "Talking about Nicki like this is hard," he says, "because she was such a part of our lives that she feels like she's still here. Nicki kept us all on track, heard all our problems, helped us get where we wanted to go. Nobody was more dedicated, committed, harder-charging. And then something happened to change all that. She got sick? Yes, that happened, but that's not what changed her. What happened was, she met Michael."

Michael, sitting between his parents and mine, smiles just a little.

Eric goes on. "Michael and Nicki together became one person, and from the day they met, that was a fact. And from then on, for Nicki, it was all about Michael, and their marriage. Her illness never consumed her. Her love did. We should all be so lucky."

As he's talking, I notice there are some beautiful flower arrangements. Mom's roses, Michael's gardenias, a nosegay from Justin. And a big, expensive-looking basket from Avery, Gardener and Brown. That's the one that gets to me the most. Why? Because it reminds me of what could have been. In another world, I might have taken the job at the law firm, worked eighteen-hour days as an intern, then moved into a junior position, and so on up the ranks. Maybe I'd have made partner some day. I might have had a marriage, a child, but I know my time would have been spent in an office, focusing on my work. In that other world, people don't know how to live. For me to learn, it took dying. And Michael. I'll put it to you: which would you choose—a life without living, or a death full of loving?

When it's over, Michael walks over and places something with the flowers—the small, smooth skipping stone, which I'd brought back from Greece and kept in my jewelry box. For luck.

Six months later there is a Soho gallery opening. The crowd is ultra-hip, dressed in every shade of black, the women with their Kate Spade and Prada bags, the men in jeans or expensive suits. Waiters pass glasses of chilled white wine and trays of sushi. If you listen closely, you'll hear a buzz about the photographer's brilliant use of contrast, shadow, and light.

Michael, you did it.

And, guess what, Michael? You're there shaking hands and introducing yourself to critics and selling your work, and you think you're alone tonight, on your own, but you're not.

"Surprise!" In races Justin, skidding on the wood floors, followed by Kate, Dad, and Mom.

"Excuse me," Michael says to a gallery assistant, and he runs to scoop up Justin.

"Sorry we're late," says Dad as he hugs Michael. "New York traffic. We're neophytes."

"Congratulations, Michael," says Mom, kissing him. "What an incredible turnout. Your show is a huge success."

"It's Justin's first trip to a gallery," says Kate.

She hands him a box of crayons and some paper. "You can go play or draw if you want while the grown-ups talk. OK?"

"Cool!" He grabs the crayons and scampers off.

Dad puts his arm around Michael. "Your parents coming?"

"Next week. I was too nervous to have them here for the opening," says Michael.

Nervous—well, that's one way to put it, Michael. And, the fact is, you look pretty confident. But you can't fool me. I know you're starting to pull away again, withdraw, so you won't be hurt. And we can't let that happen. Because, believe me, my love, you're not alone.

You'll see.

"How're you doing?" Dad asks.

"I'm—managing, thanks, Dan." He hands him a program. "Did you see? The show is dedicated to Nicki."

"That's wonderful, Michael. She would have liked that."

"Michael! Michael!" Justin runs up and pulls him by the hand. "It's Nicki!" He drags Michael through the crowd to a wall where my picture is displayed. It's one of me on the boat, and underneath is a little sticker: Not for Sale.

"I miss Nicki," says Justin.

"Me too." Michael ruffs his hair.

"But it's OK," Justin says. He reaches over and hugs Michael's legs, which are about as high as he can reach.

"See?"

"See what?" asks Michael, bending down to hug him back.

Justin looks up into his eyes. "It's just like Nicki said. If you love someone and you give them a big hug and think of them, they're always with you, hugging you back." He reaches into his pocket and hands Michael a folded-up piece of paper.

"For me?"

Justin nods vigorously. "I made it."

Michael carefully unfolds each corner of the paper. In the center is a drawing, in full crayon color: a rainbow heart.

"See?" says Justin, smiling now.

Michael stares at the heart. "Yes, Jus, I do see."

He takes the rainbow heart and tacks it up under my picture, and the two of them stand there for a while, looking at the picture and the drawing. When people you love do something like that, you are so proud of them. That's how I feel, and I know they know it, too.

Michael reaches down, picks up Justin, and

lifts him onto his shoulders. Together, they walk away. Michael knows he has Justin, and he has my mom and dad. And he has me.

So, you see, that's how I know about love, death, and the important things in life. I used to wonder how all this worked, and when Michael and I would be together again, but I don't anymore, because, the truth is, Michael was right.

We have all the time in the world.